WALDHEIM AND AUSTRIA

BY THE SAME AUTHOR

A Guide to Central Europe

RICHARD BASSETT

WALDHEIM AND AUSTRIA

VIKING

VIKING
Published by the Penguin Group
Viking Penguin Inc., 40 West 23rd Street,
New York, New York 10010, U.S.A.
Penguin Books Ltd, 27 Wrights Lane,
London W8 5TZ, England
Penguin Books Australia Ltd, Ringwood,
Victoria, Australia
Penguin Books Canada Ltd, 2801 John Street,
Markham, Ontario, Canada L3R 1B4
Penguin Books (N.Z.) Ltd, 182–190 Wairau Road,
Auckland 10, New Zealand

Penguin Books Ltd, Registered Offices:
Harmondsworth, Middlesex, England

First American Edition
Published in 1989 by Viking Penguin Inc.

1 3 5 7 9 10 8 6 4 2

Illustration credits appear on pages 6 and 7.

LIBRARY OF CONGRESS CATALOGING IN PUBLICATION DATA
Bassett, Richard.
Waldheim and Austria.
I. World War, 1939–1945—Austria. 2.Waldheim,
Kurt. 3. World War, 1939–1945—Atrocities.
4. Austria—Politics and government—1945–
I. Title.
D802.A9B37 1989 940.53'436 88-40305
ISBN 0-670-82173-X

Printed in the United States of America by
Arcata Graphics, Fairfield, Pennsylvania
Set in Ehrhardt

CONTENTS

CONTENTS

LIST OF ILLUSTRATIONS

LIST OF ILLUSTRATIONS

ACKNOWLEDGMENTS

It is my pleasure to thank the staff of the National Library, including Herr Werner Rotter, for their help in tracing archives concerning Austria's pre-war history and the fate of many resistance movements. I am grateful also to the staff of the Vienna Haus Hof and Staatarchiv and to Frau Dr Pepelka of the Heeresgeschichtliches Museum.

Also in Vienna, I owe much to long conversations with Herr Gottfried Pils, Professor Georg Eisler and Dr Georg Hofman Ostenhof. Though they are unlikely to agree with my reading of recent events in Austria, I shall always be thankful for their patience and assistance. Equally helpful was the Vienna Editor of *Die Kleine Zeitung*, Herr Kurt Vorhofer, and Hubertus Czernin of the Austrian magazine *Profil*.

I am also happy to thank Miss Patricia Howard, who made many invaluable suggestions, and Mr George Brock and Mr Michael Knipe, Foreign Editor and Foreign News Editor respectively of *The Times*, who showed great understanding for the demands this book made on my time.

Vienna, 1987
Warsaw, 1988

INTRODUCTION

For six hot months in 1986 the media of the Western world cast an unwelcome spotlight on the affairs of the small neutral republic of Austria.

For the first time since the war the Austrians found themselves the unwilling focus of the activities of the international press. For the first time since the 1930s that focus revealed an entirely different image of the country which had so long been associated in the popular mind with *Sachertorte*, Mozart and dirndls. A cupboard, which many Austrians had worked for years to keep closed, suddenly opened and among the skeletons which fell out was the hitherto undisclosed wartime career of one Lieutenant Kurt Waldheim.

Though Dr Waldheim had spent several years as Secretary-General of the United Nations, it was only when he ran for the Austrian presidency in 1986 that allegations that he had committed atrocities in the Balkans during the war began to fly.

The controversy has shown little sign of abating. To the complicated issue of whether Waldheim was involved in atrocities was added the question of the attitude of his generation in Austria towards the war and towards the Jews. Under the merciless scrutiny of the media, neither Dr Waldheim nor the Austrians have stood up particularly well. Anti-Semitism reared its ugly head during the presidential campaign, and some old wounds, which many had hoped were long forgotten, were opened once again. Austria's reputation in the world plummeted to such an extent that one distinguished British paper could accuse the country of no longer enjoying the right to stand with the West, while in the USA a veteran correspondent indulged in unprecedented vituperation by referring to the Austrians as a 'nation of pariahs'.

This book does not attempt to place either Dr Waldheim or the Austrians on trial; it would be inappropriate for a foreign correspondent to undertake such a formidable task. Rather it is an attempt to chart Austrian attitudes to traumas, which the country will be living with at least until the end of the century. Why did so many Austrians vote for Waldheim? How could a country be so indifferent to international opinion? Why, in contrast to the West Germans, have so few Austrians come to terms with their history? Are they anti-Semites and Nazis who believe their country's finest hour to have been its 1938 degradation to a province of the German Reich?

As a correspondent working in Vienna for *The Times*, I was in a privileged position and enjoyed stall seats for the events which provoked these questions. Having learnt German in Austria and been familiar with the country for years, I was uncomfortably aware of the inability of many of my Austrian friends to comprehend Waldheim's dilemma.

It was Wickham Steed, *The Times'* correspondent in Vienna before the First World War and in whose grim shadow all *Times* Vienna correspondents write, who acknowledged the Austrians' delight in the 'apotheosis of unreality'. No capital city in the world exudes such a baroque detachment from reality as Vienna. If the world found it difficult to understand the Austrians, there can be no doubt that the Austrians were completely incapable of understanding the world. What, they would ask, is all the fuss about?

What indeed? As in all fundamental questions of the political present, the answer lies in the past and, in this case, in the unhappy years of the 1930s, which moulded a generation. Few Austrians can view them with either detachment or coolness. Such qualities are unusual among the Austrians at any time, but here they may perhaps be forgiven for lacking objectivity.

In the spring of 1938 Austria confronted the inferno.

CHAPTER ONE

INFELIX *AUSTRIA*

The Austria Dr Waldheim and his contemporaries grew up in was without question a chaotic and unstable place. While for almost the first and, some would say, last time in its history Vienna and Salzburg became fashionable points of relaxation on every wealthy Englishman's summer European itinerary, putsches, terrorism and even civil war provided a bizarre counterpoint to evenings of *Kongresstanzt* and *Schuhplattler*

In the years following the break-up in 1919 of the Habsburg empire after the First World War, Austria went through every possible trauma a former great power could endure. Raging inflation reduced family savings overnight. Recession made almost half a million (out of a population of barely seven million) unemployed. Socialists and Catholics despised each other, and confrontations between them were sometimes violent.

Unfortunately, Austrians found a refuge from this chaos in armed organizations: either the pro-socialist *Schutzbund*, which was particularly strong in Vienna, or the Catholic *Heimwehr*, which represented the more conservative provinces. Though the latter was led by the charismatic but ultimately unintelligent Prince Starhemberg, the man who first coined the phrase 'Austro-Fascist', it was never a Nazi organization. Some of its supporters were, however, sympathetic to the Nazi cause. In Salzburg, which was always pro-German in sentiment, having been part of Austria only since the early nineteenth century, the *Heimwehr* leader was Goering's brother-in-law.

When Hitler became Chancellor of Germany in 1933, Nazi pressure on the small republic inevitably increased, and the undermining of Austrian morale began in earnest. Hitler was assisted by two historical factors, which had and, indeed, still have a far-reaching effect on the shaping of Austrian economic and political thinking. First, the rump of empire which was left to Austria after 1919 was that part of the Habsburgs' lands which was the least profitable. Before the creation of Czechoslovakia, Austria's industries had been situated largely in Bohemia. With the establishment of the republic of Czechoslovakia in 1918, Vienna lost all access to these, and the creation of Yugoslavia and the regime of Admiral Horthy in Hungary meant that access to much of her mineral and agricultural wealth was lost as well. Somehow Austria had to survive, but, even in Britain, few financial experts knew quite how. As for the Austrians, the future was an unknown quantity best not thought too closely about. 'The situation is hopeless but not serious,' runs a timeless Viennese adage.

Secondly, in addition to these economic factors, there was the absence in the country of any political tradition of parliamentary democracy. For centuries the Habsburgs had ruled Austria through absolutism and through a bureaucracy which fully satisfied the need of Austrians –

no less apparent today – to be administered rather than governed. Though a form of universal suffrage existed in Austria at the beginning of this century, the Austrian parliament was a far from credible voice in the country's affairs. *The Times* of the late nineteenth century contains one report after another of its proceedings: violence often broke out between members, hunting horns and whistles were blown and little, if any, serious debate took place. The parliament which emerged from the ruins of 1918 proved, not surprisingly, unable to reconcile the opposed factions in the republic's political life. When Dollfuss, the Austrian Chancellor, dissolved parliament in 1934, it was the Western democracies which felt more outraged than the Austrians, who in most cases had never taken the neo-Grec Parliament on the Ring particularly seriously. Even today the Parliament building is dwarfed by the altogether more bombastic architecture of the Town Hall, which is certainly more active and is regarded more highly than the Parliament.

In the 1930s the Austrians could perhaps be forgiven such diffidence towards the benefits of parliamentary democracy. To the north in Germany, to the south in Italy and Yugoslavia, to the east in Hungary, the message was the same: Europe was increasingly not the place for parliaments or democracy.

But if parliament was emasculated and the country's economy in dire straits, under the Dollfuss administration there was also a contempt for the Nazis, which was at first capable of preventing German propaganda from gaining any footholds in the country. The Germans too were anathema to the Austrians. Referred to traditionally as the *Piefke*, after the hapless Prussian caricature in an operetta, their very accents and direct way of approaching life created a barrier, which the brotherhood of a common language has dispelled only in the emergency of war.

The Catholic majority of the Austrian peasantry stood firmly behind Dollfuss and the Christian Social Party, which, of all the Austrian parties, believed in an independent Austria, albeit *in extremis* a conservative, fascist one. Dr Waldheim's father, and he himself as a well brought-up Catholic, supported this party. His membership of the Christian Democrat Youth Movement, like those of thousands of Austrians, represented a certain faith in a Catholic Austria; the Nazis had made no secret of their wish to destroy that faith.

But the murder of Dollfuss by the Nazis in July 1934, an assassination assisted by Austrian incompetence as well as by Austrian conspirators supporting Hitler, soon made even Catholic Austrians realize what odds were stacked against the republic's survival. The new Chancellor, Kurt von Schuschnigg, a Jesuit-educated former subaltern in the valiant Tyrolean Kaiserjaeger regiment, which had fought so tenaciously in the First World War, almost rose to the occasion, but as the storm-clouds gathered, his position became more and more hopeless. The prospects confronting the Chancellor were enough to daunt the most experienced statesman. The whole country was threatened with civil war, and to the north a powerful and avaricious neighbour was engaged in a destabilization exercise, which, if still rejected by most Austrians at this stage, slowly began to be seen, after years of weariness, as a possible solution.

For as well as contempt for the Germans, most Austrians also feel a grudging respect for a people who throughout their history have generally conducted their affairs, especially on the battlefield, with an efficiency which has so often eluded the Austrians. Even today in Austria, while one may make fun of the old imperial army of the First World War and earlier, which was defeated by virtually every army in Europe, it is much more dangerous sport to make fun of the German Wehrmacht. 'That was no operetta army! The Germans know how to make war. Best soldiers in the world,' a not so old Austrian diplomat once exclaimed to me, flushed with pride.

If Waldheim and his generation of young men in Austria were too young to have had any personal experience of German efficiency, there were plenty of people – all those who were over the age of thirty-five in the late 1930s – who could recall what war allied to the Germans was about. As has been well documented elsewhere, from 1917 the Austrian General Staff was little more than an appendage to the decisions of German military thinking. From Romania across Galicia to the Italian front, what victories there were took place only with the stiffening of several German divisions with Austrian soldiers.

This almost love–hate, perhaps rather closer to contempt–respect, relationship the Austrians have with the Germans is still visible today. The extravagant racial mix of the Austrians, most of whom had Slav or Magyar or some Jewish blood in them, created psychological tensions among a people whose culture and traditions were for centuries expressed exclusively in German.

It should not be forgotten that Dr Waldheim's family name was originally Czech – Waclavek – and that, like thousands of Slavs, his family believed their chances of advancement in the monarchy were improved by Germanizing their names. It is still deeply embedded in the psyches of many Austrians that to be a Slav is to be some form of second-class citizen. Among some so-called educated Austrians it is even considered acceptable to refer to people from Yugoslavia as *Untermenschen* (subhuman). While, of course, such comments are only representative of a small minority, the general dislike of Slavs is widespread and particularly strong in Vienna; this is ironic, given the Slav appearance which betrays the non-German origins of so many Austrians.

If such feelings were not themselves enough to undermine totally Austria's self-confidence in the 1930s, the country also had to put up with economic sanctions from neighbouring Germany. As western Austria, especially the Tyrol and Salzburg, was dependent on tourism for its income, Nazi Germany was in a position to devastate the Austrian economy simply by taxing all Germans visiting Austria and so cutting immediately the number of German tourists by over half.

Chancellor Schuschnigg, all too aware that as far as the Germans were concerned the Anschluss, or annexation, was already becoming an economic reality, attempted to rally foreign opinion. This proved, however, far from easy. In Britain, a government pursuing appeasement had little time for the German-speaking Austrian desire to be independent of Nazi Germany. Attempts by opposition politicians to persuade the Prime Minister, Neville Chamberlain, to 'express the hope' that Austria's affairs be conducted 'without foreign pressure and interference' from Germany were shouted down in parliament by most Conservative MPs. Since economic experts in Britain foresaw little chance of Austria surviving without Germany and since the government chose to remain silent when asked whether it would support a German invasion, there was obviously little comfort for Schuschnigg in London. It was not just the government which was unfavourably disposed towards him. Even the Labour Party, knowing that a couple of years earlier Schuschnigg's party had backed the bombardment of socialists in the civil war, offered a pretty frosty reception.

With France, the power which at a meeting with Italy and Britain at Stresa in 1935 had agreed to keep a watchful eye over Austria, Schuschnigg fared little better. If France through a series of alliances in Eastern Europe believed it could contain Germany, it was wishful thinking which bore no relation to its actual military power. In the 1930s, as was to be made quickly clear, France could not logistically fulfil any obligations in Central and Eastern Europe; her forces were hopelessly disorganized and incapable of offensive campaigning.

The Führer, himself an Austrian, knew that even Italy would not raise a finger to prevent him reclaiming the country of his birth. Though the powers of Western

Europe underestimated the importance of Austria as the key to South-eastern Europe, Hitler did not. The promises made by the three-power front formed at Stresa regarding any threat to Austria's independence came to nothing. Isolated abroad, undermined at home, Schuschnigg's Austria now moved swiftly towards extinction.

In February 1938 Schuschnigg consented to meet Hitler in Berchtesgaden, the Führer's 'eagle's nest' perched high in the Alps in a pocket of Germany which is still bordered on three sides by Austrian territory. Here the Austrian Chancellor was browbeaten and abused for hours as the Führer raved and cursed. When Schuschnigg, who smoked heavily, reached for a cigarette, Hitler shrieked that he never allowed smoking in his presence. To his credit, Schuschnigg lit the cigarette and, with raised eyebrows, tossed the match on to a nearby table. Unless Austria followed Germany's foreign policy and domestic anti-Semitic legislation and gave all key ministerial positions to the Nazis, she would be crushed. To underline the point Hitler showed the Chancellor a copy of Vienna's 'secret' defence plans. In return for compliance with his demands, Hitler promised to respect Austrian independence.

Schuschnigg now attempted to outflank the Nazis by suddenly calling for a plebiscite supporting a 'free independent Austria'. Perhaps Schuschnigg thought he could call Hitler's bluff. In fact, he forced the Führer's hand and invasion was put in motion. Two days before the plebiscite was to be held, Germany closed its frontier with Austria, and reports of German mobilization reached Vienna from Munich. Presumed destination: Austria.

In a farewell broadcast Chancellor Schuschnigg ordered the Austrians to offer no resistance. He said it was essential to 'avoid bloodshed in a fratricidal war'. This decision, which perhaps more than any other was to be remembered in years to come, was to cast doubt for ever on the degree of acquiescence with which the Austrians greeted the Nazis. 'Remember Belgium,' one of Schuschnigg's advisers implored. 'Remember how that country was resurrected only because it resisted as long as it could.' 'Let us fight to the last man,' observed another. Yet there was only one thing to do, Schuschnigg later wrote: 'Think clearly and act with realism to save what could be saved of our country.'

Not far from the Austrian Chancellery, where Schuschnigg broadcast his speech, there stands a fine equestrian statue of the Austrian Archduke Charles, who was the first general ever to defeat Napoleon on land. More than any other monument in Austria it expresses the curious, inseparable fate of the two nations. On one side run the words: 'dedicated to the fearless leader of Austria's army'; on the other: 'who fought for Germany's honour'. Since such ambivalence towards a powerful neighbour had been resolved by military intimidation and instruction from above, it is perhaps not surprising that barricades did not suddenly spring up about Vienna in 1938. Moreover, unlike Czechoslovakia, Austria at this time did not possess even a hint of a modern army. A year later the Czechs, with all their splendid munitions, fell into the hands of the Nazis without firing any shots, so perhaps the Austrians may be excused for bowing to the inevitable.

Not that the inevitable was taken on the chin by all. In Tyrol, traditionally the most independently minded part of the country, with a long tradition of freedom-fighting, which had cost the Bavarians and Napoleon dearly in the nineteenth century, some shots were exchanged. At Hall some Austrian soldiers defied Schuschnigg's orders and a small skirmish took place. (Although the evidence for this particular incident rests only on personal accounts, for the Germans were quick to destroy the official report, British military intelligence was satisfied that some resistance had occurred.)

But a few shots ringing out among the medieval buildings of Hall are a pathetic gesture of defiance. It is to be regretted that, despite Schuschnigg's capitulation in Vienna, the ranks of Austria's monarchists, Jews, socialists and patriots could not have produced a few more fanatics in the mountainous territory of western Austria, which is so suited to guerrilla warfare. None the less, as has been pointed out by Gordon Brooke-Shepherd in his admirable study of these years, *The Austrian Odyssey* (London, Macmillan, 1957), a nation can be pitied for not producing martyrs, but it cannot be blamed for it. If in March 1938 Austria had no cause to be proud of her behaviour, neither had she any particular reason to be embarrassed. And in this she is one up on the rest of Europe.

How the Austrians behaved after the Anschluss is another matter. As the envoys of the Western democracies swiftly converted their legations into consulates to condone the rape, so the Austrian Catholic Church saw little difficulty in overcoming its earlier objections to the godless Reich. The Austrian Catholic Bench of Bishops, headed by Cardinal Innitzer, issued a proclamation expressing 'innermost conviction and free will' and praising the 'splendid services of Nazism in the social field . . . We expect all Christians to proclaim themselves as Germans for the German Reich.'

There can be no doubt that, like thousands of other Austrian Catholics, Dr Waldheim also 'welcomed' the Anschluss. The previous year he had enrolled at the University of Vienna, where he began to study law. As a former officer in an Austrian cavalry regiment, there can be no doubt that he was fully aware of Austria's inability to resist the German Wehrmacht. Like most Austrians, he was forced to swim with the tide and hope for the best, believing that somehow Austria would be spared from the nastiness of the Nazis.

Vienna's fatalistic approach to events was less evident in Salzburg. Swastikas were soon to be seen everywhere for, as Osbert Lancaster observed, though the *Hochwohlgeborene* on the Wolfgangsee might speak of the *Reichsdeutsche* only with the most profound distaste, when it came to the crunch, most of them experienced small difficulty in overcoming their fastidiousness.

Nor were Catholics and Counts alone in supporting the Anschluss. Even the former socialist Chancellor, Dr Karl Renner, could declare to the demoralized Austro-Marxists, who a few years earlier had been capable of recruiting several young Englishmen, including Philby, to the cause, that 'the wandering of the Austrian people is now ended and it returns united to the starting-point set out in its solemn declaration of November 12 1918. The sad intermezzo of the half century 1866 [the Austro-Prussian war]–1918 thus becomes submerged in our thousand years of common history.' *Sic transit* Austria.

At a new plebiscite on 10 April an overwhelming 99.7 per cent was in favour of the Anschluss. Even allowing for the fact that Goebbels staged the event, there was probably an overwhelming majority. As to the true balance between support for and acquiescence and opposition to the Anschluss at that time, we are fortunate in possessing the only source which could afford to be objective in 1938, the Nazis' own intelligence.

On 20 June 1938, less than three months after the invasion, the Gestapo at Innsbruck compiled for their headquarters in Vienna a confidential estimate of the current state of pro-German sympathies in the Tyrol. The original of this document survived all the chaos of war and Allied occupation, and it offers an illuminating picture of the Ostmark, as the Austrian part of the Reich was called. It is, needless to say, a view which was never permitted to appear in the Nazi propaganda machine.

The survey divides the Tyroleans into four strata of political reliability, arranged in descending order of their enthusiasm for the cause. The first group – the 'faithful fighters and totally reliable National Socialists' – is estimated as forming 'at the most 15 per cent'. Beyond this hard core there is a section of Nazis who are 'opportunists' and are toeing the party line out of spite rather than conviction. Opposed to the Jews and the clerical regime of Schuschnigg, they are found to form 30 per cent. A further 20 per cent is categorized as being 'occasional supporters': Austrians who felt drawn at times to some aspects of the Nazi programme, but who remained during and after the Anschluss 'uncertain and unreliable' *in extremis*. The remaining 35 per cent is perceived as being made up of 'open or hidden opponents of the movement'. Though the opposition of this group is 'concealed in indifference' for the most part, its members are said to be 'clearly hostile and spiteful'. Thus, while almost two thirds of the Austrians might at one time embrace the swastika, their degree of commitment varied. As the compiler of the report acknowledged, 'We must not allow the results of the 99.7 per cent plebiscite vote to mislead us.'

Cases of token resistance at this time were rare, but three familiar to the author will suffice to show that not all Austrians in 1938 were committed Nazis. The first concerns a remarkable academic in the Tyrol, a man whose knowledge of different languages and passion for Esperanto made him one of the most interesting tutors at the University of Innsbruck. Aged twenty-three, with a brilliant doctorate behind him and, as was carefully researched by the Nazis, not a drop of Jewish blood in his family, he was clearly officer material. But the young doctor, though fit – he had recently cycled from Copenhagen to Istanbul – had absolutely no desire to serve in the German Wehrmacht. It was quickly brought home to him that there was little choice in the matter. Present yourself for conscription or you will be *radikal ausgewiesen*, a not very subtle euphemism for the concentration camp or execution for treason.

A streak of Tyrolean obstinacy and independence asserted itself, like that which had inspired the forgotten garrison commander at Hall. For four years this young man lived from hand to mouth in the western Alps, avoiding the Nazi patrols which were ordered to bring him back dead or alive. Today he readily admits his contempt for the Nazis and for his fellow Austrians who blindly followed them, but he also acknowledges that many passively resisted them and that on more than one occasion he owed his life to such unsung heroes who concealed him.

Count T. was also perfect officer material. Six-feet-six with blond Aryan looks, educated at Oxford, where he was a contemporary of Harold Acton, he seemed an obvious supporter of the cause. But the Count too, though he had served in the *Heimwehr* – 'we always interrupted our dinners to look for Nazi saboteurs, but more often only found some English deb in a Delahaye lost on the road' – had little sympathy for the Germans.

The morning the Germans marched into Vienna, he was attending a meeting at the Haus der Industriellen Vereinigung in the Schwarzenberg Platz. A motion was quickly passed welcoming the Anschluss and the 'Heil Hitler' salute rang out among the wealthy nervous industrialists. Only three people failed to give the salute: two were Jewish and the third was the Count. On entering his club at lunch it was quickly made apparent that this gesture had not gone unnoticed. 'It seemed as if the entire club had nothing better to do but discuss why I had not given the salute,' the Count recalled. It was clear that Vienna and, indeed, Austria was no place for him, so, taking his life into his hands, he decided to leave. It required courage and nerve, especially as the borders were strictly controlled, but, by heading for Germany rather than Prague, he disarmed suspicions and eventually made it to Belgium and South America.

A third Austrian, then only nineteen, possessed less self-confidence and, like most of his contemporaries, gave himself up to the Wehrmacht's conscription lists. Some forty years later he remains deeply ashamed that he was not capable of sterner resistance. He describes how, by greeting each other with '*Gruss Gott*' rather than 'Heil Hitler', Austrians who did not wholeheartedly support the Reich indulged in a form of passive resistance. During the war they adopted a policy of 'always firing above the enemies' heads except when they were obviously going to kill you'. Implausible and pathetic though this all seems, it was at least a gesture, albeit typically Austrian in its unrealistic approach to life.

Whatever Dr Waldheim's role in the Balkans in the early 1940s, one thing is abundantly clear: he did not follow any of the three routes of token resistance described above. On the other hand, the fact that after four years of wartime service he rose no higher than lieutenant speaks for a certain lack of commitment to the cause. The same intelligence reports which had so critically examined the depth of the Tyroleans' loyalty to the Nazis were extremely sceptical of young Waldheim, whose family was repeatedly interrogated on account of its anti-Nazi beliefs. It may well be that by showing enthusiasm for the Nazis, Waldheim hoped to spare his family further trials. It is equally possible, though, that like many Austrians at that time, he believed his parents to be mistaken and the future to lie with the glorious thousand-year Reich.

Between the two extremes of enthusiasm and resistance stood the shifting mass of opportunists and waverers eager to prove their worth to their new masters. The Austrian leadership, with the sole exception of President Miklas, who insisted 'The Germans cannot tell me what to do', abdicated all responsibility. With Schuschnigg yielding to the first German ultimatum and three other politicians turning down his vacant post, Austria was as abandoned by her statesmen as by the Western powers.

Meanwhile, in Vienna, the 'brown' flood swept through the streets; it was an 'indescribable witches' sabbath', as G. E. R. Gedye, former correspondent for *The Times* in Vienna, recalled a year later. 'I walked through the mobs whose faces called for the pencil of a Gustav Doré; one of the many sentimental phrases applied by the Viennese to themselves mockingly halted my brain – "*Das gold'ne Wiener Herz*". There was little trace of golden hearts written on these hate-filled, triumph-drunken faces, and the memory of it makes one's stomach queasy.' In the Leopoldstadt, where the majority of Vienna's 200,000 Jews lived, the terror was unlimited. 'Now day after day, Nazi storm-troopers, surrounded by jostling, jeering and laughing mobs of "golden Viennese hearts", dragged Jews from shops, offices and homes, men and women, put scrubbing brushes in their hands, splashed them well with acid and made them go down on their knees.' As Gedye noted, on the day of Hitler's triumphal entry into Vienna the suicide rate rose to three figures, and the daily average did not sink below it for many weeks. Whenever it showed signs of slackening, some new order would be issued to stamp despair deeper into the hearts of the Nazis' victims. 'The sweep of the Nazi scythe continued to cut down ruthlessly the flower of the intellectual and professional life in Vienna, impatient to destroy the last traces of that cultured civilization which for five years had marked out the distinction between Austria and Germany.'

The entire ghastly drama was re-enacted a few months later in the Sudetenland when, with Chamberlain's compliance at Munich, the Germans marched into Czechoslovakia. As a reserve officer, Dr Waldheim was assigned to the German occupation of the Sudetenland at the beginning of October 1938. Some months after the events in Vienna, he could no longer have been in any doubt about what the Nazis were up to. The month before he had been at Dobritz near Berlin, where he attended the cavalry school. He could not have failed to notice what was happening in the Reich and that he was serving a monstrous machine. 'I only did my duty' were the words he used to describe this and his later service in the German Wehrmacht. Performing one's duty came to be equated with accepting the extinction of Austria as a free state.

Perhaps the running-down of the red-white-red colours of the country in 1938 seemed less important – as one unrepentant Nazi once told me – than the sudden granting of a widow's pension which for years had been denied by Austrian inefficiency. Perhaps the ill-treatment of the Jews was overshadowed by the sudden possibility of wider markets for trade, smarter uniforms and the chance to be part of a 'big operation' once again. Perhaps the brutality was just a temporary price which had to be paid and the Austrians would soon be able to rule their own *Gau* without interference from the Germans. The Austrians were shortly to be disabused of any such ideas. As we shall see, by giving rein to their traditional anti-Semitism, they had sold their souls to the devil, and a full price was to be exacted.

CHAPTER TWO

RESISTING THE NAZIS

There is something in the Austrian character, perhaps a legacy of baroque times, which delights in excess; few people north of the Alps can be moved to a state of hysteria as easily as the Austrians. In 1938 more than one observer was struck by the fanaticism with which Austrians reacted to the occasion. But as if intoxicated by bad wine, the Austrians' dream was swiftly replaced by a reality which no one but the most fervent Austrian Nazis could have found palatable.

The Austrian capacity for self-deception, the *Leichte-begeisterungsfähigheit*, was never more rudely shattered than during these days. Many Austrians who believed in the Nazi creed were shaken by what followed the Anschluss. Far from there being a respected Austrian state within the Reich, the country was immediately turned into one of the Reich's *Gaue*, or provinces. Far from there being more power for local Austrian Nazis, the long corridors in the Herrengasse resounded to hard north German accents as an army of reliable Prussian bureaucrats was brought in to administer the new province.

If the Austrian Nazis were dismayed by this, the Austrians who detested the new order were horrified. Those who were prepared to do more than just concentrate on the all-consuming business of saving their own skins began to organize themselves into resistance movements from the beginning. The story of Austrian resistance during the war is, in true Central European style, closer to operetta than serious drama. None the less, given the conditions any Austrian wishing to resist the Nazis had to face, those who seek to dismiss its role are misguided. One may look in vain for the heroic, almost suicidal, courage of the *maquis* or the Poles. At the same time, the Austrians were operating in an entirely different scenario.

For many Austrians the common language and the closeness of race and culture meant that the Germans, though they might be despised, could never be hated in the way the French loathed *le sale Boche*. The common tongue made underground activity particularly hazardous. And there was the Austrians' characteristic inability to resist the tide. Compound this with a predilection for fatalism and resigning oneself to one's fate, together with an inherent antipathy towards logistics, and the reason why the Austrian resistance lacked any cohesion is swiftly apparent. As Gordon Brooke-Shepherd observes, the Austrian resistance was remarkable more for what it tried to do than for what it failed to do.

Within the first ten days of the Nazi occupation some 90,000 Austrians were rounded up by the Gestapo, which made any underground activity dangerous. But on the very night that the Nazis marched into Vienna resistance *was* under way. It would be incorrect to suggest that it was either widespread or particularly important, but it should not be forgotten. Some people paid for it with their lives.

On the Left the communists proved the most dedicated

and fanatic. The socialists, though less extreme, at least drew strength from the fact that they believed not in some world dictatorship of the proletariat but in a socialist Austria. The socialists' resistance was often passive. 'Do the job far worse than anyone else' was their saying, and while such resistance is less dramatically heroic than armed conflict, its effect should not be underestimated. Some 90 per cent of the Vienna fire brigade was socialist in sympathy, and their unreliability sufficiently impressed the Gestapo for them to transport half the entire brigade (730 men) to the army firing range at Kagran to witness the execution of two of their comrades for 'treason'.

Austrian patriotism from the beginning, however, was more eagerly grasped by the Right. Whether priests, students, monarchists, peasants or officers, these Austrians were fortified by two things denied their Marxist colleagues: respect for Austria's traditions and devotion to the Catholic Church. At first their activities were tinged with theatre. Students gathered on the Leopoldsberg above Vienna, forming the Grey Free Corps. They had originally gathered machine-guns, but after Schuschnigg's broadcast capitulating to the Nazis, they resorted to daubing walls with anti-Nazi slogans and removing swastikas. Brave dilettantism was no match for the Gestapo and within weeks their leaders were dispatched to Dachau.

Monarchist cells fared a little better. The first was penetrated by the Gestapo only after six months. Its leader, Captain Burian, was executed in March 1944. Another, led by the Augustine monk Karl Scholz, managed to recruit 400 members, but its activities were undermined by the Catholic Bench of Bishops, who were busy preaching conciliation with the Nazis in Vienna, a few miles down the Danube from Scholz's abbey at Klosterneuburg. Less romantic but equally ineffectual was a group formed around a lawyer, Dr Jakob Kastelic, whose supporters dreamt of a Catholic federation of the Danube. In the summer of 1940 this and other monarchist groups were betrayed to the Gestapo, which arrested 240 of its activists. Nine of the leaders, including the monk Scholz, were executed, another nine died in prison.

By 1941, then, it was clear to Austrians of every political creed that if resistance to the Nazis was going to have any effect, differences between the various anti-Nazi groups would have to be settled. Common distaste for the occupation and a whiff of long-overdue Austrian patriotism were the bonds which helped the former propaganda chief of the Austrian Chancellor Dollfuss (who had been murdered by the Nazis), Hans Becker, to set up his anti-Nazi 'bureau'. Under his organization cells throughout the country began to engage in a four-point programme: factory sabotage; resistance and sabotage of the Wehrmacht recruitment system; patriotic propaganda; and co-operation with underground groups in neighbouring countries.

Becker was undeterred by the practical problems of organizing resistance in Austria. 'The non-existence of our state should on no account lead us to neglect an Austrian foreign policy,' he bravely said in 1942 when signs of any change in Austria's fate seemed as remote as ever. On the basis of Becker's Central Committee for Austria a group emerged, which if little more than a symbol, succeeded in presenting Austrians and the world with confirmation that resistance was possible. The O5 organization came into existence during the winter of 1944–5. Its name was little more than a dramatic inspiration, but the night after it had been agreed upon it appeared on the walls of every suburb in Vienna. Within a week an entire Gestapo section was established to bring the organization to book.

It was thanks largely to the persistence of Fritz Molden, the distinguished Austrian publisher, that the Allies came to know of the organization. While serving with the Wehrmacht in Italy, Molden established communications with the partisans. By January 1945 he had contacted all four Allies to seek recognition for the Austrian underground.

A new incentive towards resistance had been provided, not by the Nazis but by the Russians, through the Moscow declaration of November 1943, which was broadcast to the Austrians; it made known to the world that in the final settlement of Austria's future 'account will inevitably be taken of her own contribution to her liberation'. Before this statement was made, little co-ordinated resistance had taken place in Austria, and what underground movements there were failed to score any runs. But the organizations, however badly led or ineffectual, did exist. Inevitably, after Stalingrad, and America's entry into the war, the organizations became stronger. By the spring of 1945 O5 had successfully penetrated the Vienna police, Vienna radio and most of the power industries in the city. Moreover, some 1,500 activists were armed and began carrying out attacks on SS (*Schutzstaffel*) personnel in Vienna. In the four-week period between January 21 and February 24, 1945, thirty-six SS men were killed. In retaliation seventeen O5 members were shot and scores more were captured and imprisoned. The Gestapo raided the Committee's offices and arrested the most valuable members, including Becker. O5 never really recovered from this, but by then the torch of resistance in Austria had passed to another organization, which had also engaged in 'resistance': the Austrian army.

From the first day of the German occupation the Austrian officer corps had been regarded with great suspicion. The heirs to the traditions of Frederick the Great were not slow in showing their contempt for the Austrians. Western correspondents still *en poste* in Vienna when the Nazis marched in were treated to the extraordinary spectacle of a German lieutenant threatening a group of Austrian staff officers with a pistol on the steps of the Chancellery. But, as with the Catholic Church in Austria, resistance to the Nazis came from the bottom. The first known cell was formed in 1939 by a group of Austrian NCOs serving in Vienna under the leadership of one Sergeant Franz Studeny. Its aims were not particularly ambitious. Rather than foolishly provoking reprisals by any sudden act of sabotage, it merely set about recruiting as many people as possible for potential future action.

As the war progressed, Studeny made contact with a group of junior army officers, including Captain Szokoll, who worked in close contact with German army dissidents under the ill-fated Count von Stauffenberg. Szokoll went for talks with Stauffenberg in 1942 and military co-ordination for the July plot against Hitler was arranged through another Austrian, Colonel Bernardis.

Much time and space has been devoted to the German officers under Stauffenberg who attempted to assassinate Hitler and preserve a future for the Fatherland. Vienna was by no means under-represented in this most spectacular attempt on Hitler's life. Indeed, such is the irony of history that while Stauffenberg and his Prussian officers botched the job, in Vienna Szokoll and his men acted with most unusual precision. Within one hour of receipt of the agreed telegram announcing the emergency decisions following Hitler's supposed death, the Austrians in the plot moved. All the garrisons in the two provinces of the Lower Danube were alerted. Before two hours had passed they were already busy taking over the administration from the SS. Several of the most important Nazi commanders in the city were arrested and taken to the former Imperial War Ministry, a gaunt overpowering building on the Ringstrasse. These included the deputy *Gauleiter*, Scharitzer, the SS General Querner, the local head of propaganda, Frauenfeld, and the President of the Vienna police, Gotzmann. Each one of these important links in the Nazi chain of command in Vienna was placed under guard in solitary confinement.

Szokoll was in the process of issuing orders for the dissolution of the SS when news of the putsch's failure arrived. Those who were involved and survived recalled later that Szokoll reached Stauffenberg on the phone and asked for instructions. Before the line was cut, Stauffenberg's last words were: 'Don't say you are letting me down too?'

By the time Szokoll returned to the main office, the SS chiefs who had been incarcerated and had doubtless feared the worst were eagerly telephoning their offices with orders to arrest all the Austrians on their files. Within the next few hours every Austrian with aristocratic connections serving in the Wehrmacht in Vienna was dismissed. Hundreds were arrested; many of them were executed, including Count Marogna-Redwitz, the head of regional intelligence and a close collaborator of Admiral Canaris.

Szokoll himself was spared. Unbetrayed and unsuspected – he had after all acted on orders from Berlin – this patriot turned immediately to a new ruse in resistance. A new plan for an independent Viennese revolt was now devised under the code-name 'Radetzky'.

By the beginning of 1945, thanks to an ingenious system of cross-posting and forged returns on new Wehrmacht drafts, Szokoll, now a major, had managed to ensure that large bodies of 'patriotic Austrians' were posted to the units around Vienna. Most of the units were made up of predominantly Austrian personnel. Among them were a battalion of the Hoch and Deutschmeister regiment, a provincial infantry battalion under Major Schick, who knew the full details of the scheme, and the officers and personnel of the Vienna military police, led by Major Biedermann.

What follows is one of the most remarkable stories of the war. Resigned to the fact that his units would have to help the Russians – the Western Allies were still many miles away – Szokoll sent an NCO called Ferdinand Kaes to break through the German lines and make contact with the Russian advance guard. Through a mixture of luck, bluff and characteristically Austrian improvisation, Kaes managed to get through the battle lines and reach Marshal Tolbuchin's HQ.

Armed with intelligence as to the whereabouts of two SS divisions guarding Vienna, Kaes was finally trusted by the Russians and then returned to the German lines. But while plans for a co-ordinated stroke were being finalized by Szokoll and the Russians, an Austrian somewhere lost his nerve. As the rebel units gathered in the city centre, Major Biedermann was arrested and tortured. Before being hanged with other officers in the gloomy suburb of Floridsdorf, the Major disclosed the names of his accomplices. Szokoll's office in the War Ministry was raided, but he escaped, having been alerted to the plot's failure before he reached the Ministry. The plot had failed, but not long after, O5 agents led the Russians into the city.

It is difficult to say how many Austrians died for their country during the seven-odd years of the Nazi period. It would be folly to suggest that they were greater in number than the Austrians who died defending the Reich, but the preceding paragraphs show that Austria was by no means as secure as the Germans would have liked and that an extraordinary mixture of students, monks and NCOs were prepared to die for a country which in 1938 the West had believed could not exist except as part of a 'Greater Germany'.

Lists compiled during the war show that 4,000 Austrians were imprisoned for treason and that nearly 2,000 were executed, but they exclude all those who were sentenced without any formal trial and who were shot out of hand. The lists of names are long forgotten by a republic which has preferred collective amnesia to an impartial appraisal of these events. One records that Kurt Waldheim was not to be found on them. For him, the war was a very different affair.

Dr Waldheim served in a German Wehrmacht which had little time for any Austrian sensibilities. It may be that he, like Szokoll, engaged in the dangerous game of subversion from within, but this seems unlikely and it is certainly not suggested by any of the many versions of Dr Waldheim's movements during the war. What follows is confusing, largely as a result of Waldheim's own statements. In putting together the pieces of his military career, we must rely on evidence which seems to be constantly shifting.

Everyone agrees that from the outbreak of war Waldheim was a serving officer with the rank of cornet or sub-lieutenant, an obsolescent rank used to denote the lowest officer in a cavalry regiment. According to the President's own official record in the 'White Book' (a document produced by the Austrian Foreign Ministry in 1987), he managed to avoid the initial fighting in Poland by attending a course in Berlin. Subsequently he was on holiday with his family until 11 January 1940, when he was again away from his unit on 'study leave'.

The first active fighting he saw was during the Western campaign in May. By December 1940, despite further periods of study leave, he was commissioned and given the rank of lieutenant. In the late spring of 1941 Dr Waldheim's reconnaissance squadron was transported by train directly from France to the Eastern front to participate in the Russian campaign. He then moved through Russia with his unit and in early December 1941 he was wounded in action near Orël. From a field hospital, where he was initially treated, Dr Waldheim was sent to the war hospital at Frankfurt-an-der Oder and then flown to an army hospital in Vienna. In February 1942 he was released from the hospital for treatment as an out-patient. On 6 March 1942 he reported to the cavalry reserve unit at Stockerau. From 7 March to 7 April he was on convalescent leave with his family in Baden, a small spa town near Vienna. At this time he was classified as physically unfit for combat duty.

Subsequent assignments in several subordinate staff functions in the Balkans enabled him to spend almost one year in Austria, where he continued his studies and completed his law degree. There is less agreement on the next stage of his military career.

In his autobiography, aptly entitled *In the Eye of the Storm* (London, Weidenfeld & Nicolson, 1985) Dr Waldheim omitted to mention the following period or give details of his military activities. Though he later was to claim that his book had been drastically shortened by his publishers, it is hard not to think that the President knowingly drew a veil over this period.

At the end of his convalescent leave Dr Waldheim, who had studied Italian at the Consular Academy, was assigned to Army High Command 12. Because of the Axis forces' need for German–Italian interpreters in the Balkans, he was posted to Montenegro.

The Italian involvement in the Balkans, which included the invasion of Albania and the occupation of Montenegro, was a little theatrical. In Albania vast villas were constructed in the most up-to-date style and filled with treasures from old Italian families whose scions were among the Fascists 'of the first hour'. In Montenegro one Italian prince rashly accepted the title of King of the country, only to realize that he was the uncrowned and unloved monarch of the most warlike race in Europe.

Characteristically, he never set foot in the region. His proclamation calling for the surrender of all weapons, which was signed by the Italian *Amministrazione*, was met by the handing in of two rifles, both Italian in make, which had been 'borrowed' from two Italian sentries.

The campaign in the Balkans was certainly one of the bloodiest for the Wehrmacht. As usual, it invaded without any declaration of war. As usual, the old racial theories of Teuton superiority over Slav, which had led to the systematic decimation of Poles at the beginning of the war, were put into practice with the southern Slavs. The Slovenes of the north and the Croats, many of whom had a knowledge of German, were treated less brutally than the Serbs and Bosnians, who if they did not wish to be part of the new order which envisaged Aryan superiority, would have to take the consequences. Owing to the mountainous terrain of the Balkans, partisan resistance was feasible. As a result of the traditional martial qualities of the southern Slavs, such resistance became a reality which menaced German lines of communication almost throughout the peninsula.

There was also an exclusively Austrian side to this campaign. Professor Dennison Rusinow, in his remarkable book *Italy's Austrian Inheritance*, observes how when the Germans invaded Yugoslavia, areas of the Balkans, which had been ruled by the Habsburgs before 1918, found themselves at the mercy of their former rulers, now re-equipped and harnessed to a far more deadly machine. The Wehrmacht was certainly more professional and ruthless than anything the Austrians had fielded in imperial days. In towns and villages in Yugoslavia it was sometimes the very same officers who had once served there as subalterns who returned as commandants. The clock was thus turned grimly back.

As the fighting in this area became more and more like guerrilla warfare, the Nazis reacted with the utmost brutality towards the partisans. It is in the nature of partisan warfare that civilian casualties mount. German commanders, frustrated at every turn by an enemy which was all-seeing but mostly invisible, pursued two policies. They first encouraged collaboration, which worked very well in Croatia, a Catholic province of the federal state of Yugoslavia, which had never been happy being ruled from Belgrade. More often, however, they pursued a 'scorched earth' policy. Villages were razed; civilians were seized at random and shot.

For every German soldier shot, 100 civilians were found and executed. Often this included women and children. It was a policy which only increased the violence. Just as the Allies hoped the bombing of German cities would break the Nazis' morale, so too did the Wehrmacht, and in particular the SS, believe all that was needed to crack the partisans was the mass slaughter of their families. Both policies proved spectacularly how foolish such theories were, and in both cases feeling against the destroyer only hardened.

Dr Waldheim is at pains to point out that from the beginning of his assignment in the Balkans he was placed well behind the lines as an interpreter and was far removed from any fighting. In *The Times* (1 May 1986) he was reported as saying with regard to the partisan war, 'I know nothing.'

Though Waldheim himself has stressed the interpreting duties of his assignments, the 'White Book' admits that he also served as a liaison officer. After more leave, this time because of a thyroid condition, he re-joined the staff of Army Group E, led by another Austrian, General Löhr (later shot for war crimes by the Yugoslavs). Here, as the 'White Book' tersely notes, Dr Waldheim resumed the duties of an 03 ordnance officer assigned to the Ic (military intelligence) section. In that assignment he collated incoming military information into twice-daily enemy situation reports. Documents indicate that he had been appointed to this position in late 1943 and continued these duties until 15 August 1944, a period in excess of six months.

As is so often the case when a book is produced to whitewash someone's character, what is omitted only fuels speculation. It was left to the World Jewish Congress to fill in the gaps. They allege that German army documents signed by Waldheim prove that his daily task was the collation of intelligence reports from all outposts of Army Group E, which contained information about the partisan war and the arrest of Jews from Salonika and their transportation to death camps. Other records reveal that Waldheim had also signed interrogation reports.

On 19 August Dr Waldheim returned to Vienna to get married. Again the 'White Book' takes up its self-effacing tale: 'He remained on marriage leave until September 3 1944, when he was prematurely recalled to an 03 ordnance officer position in the Ic section of the Army Group E staff in Arsakli.' In the autumn of 1944, the situation of Army Group E had deteriorated substantially. This factor dictated the relocation of its headquarters from Arsakli to Mitrovica in Yugoslavia. Most of the officers, the book hastens to point out, accomplished this relocation by first flying from Arsakli to Priština and then motoring to the staff headquarters in Stari Trg, near Mitrovica. One month later the staff of Army Group E further withdrew to Sarajevo. Again Dr Waldheim and other staff members made the journey by aeroplane. The retreat, though accomplished in reasonably good order – Army Group E was to reach the Austrian frontier virtually intact – was accompanied by many reprisals. No doubt the fact that

Dr Waldheim was travelling largely by air protected him from any direct participation in these events. Whether as a staff officer of moderate intelligence he could claim ignorance of such events remains, however, questionable. The international historical commission set up by the Austrian government to investigate their President's wartime past found that Waldheim was 'one of the best informed officers in the Balkans'.

With the gradual collapse of the Wehrmacht, Waldheim, who once again seems to have wangled leave in Vienna, was ordered to join an infantry division near Trieste. From Zagreb, where Army Group E was reconstructing its headquarters, the easiest way to Trieste lay via Ljubljana, some 60 miles north-west, but as the partisans appear to have been in control of most of Slovenia by this time, Waldheim had to return to Austria and try to reach the port through Carinthia, a journey of over 300 miles instead of a more direct, if hazardous, route of barely 120 miles.

The journey was the last Waldheim was to do in the service of the Reich; the attempt to link two points in a straight line by the most circuitous route was an appropriate end to his wartime service. Though he tried to reach Trieste via Klagenfurt by 9 May, it appears that the end of the thousand-year Reich was so obvious that Dr Waldheim demobilized, joining his wife and child in the idyllic hills of Ramsau near the Styrian–Lower Austrian frontier. For the Oberleutnant and for millions of other Ostmarker, the war, like the Reich, was over.

CHAPTER THREE

COLLABORATORS OR VICTIMS?

Perhaps because Austria was still more closely associated with such figures as Mozart, Schubert and Haydn than with being part of Germany, the end of the war was less harsh for the Austrians than for the Germans. The Allies, whether French, British, American or Russian, seemed to treat the Austrians differently. The Austrians themselves fully exploited any mythology concerning their history which had survived seven years of obscurity in the Reich. Just as an appeasement-conscious Britain had tolerated the antics of Mussolini on the grounds that a mass of Italians dressing up in black shirts did not seem to be particularly menacing, so too were the Austrians seen as far less evil than the Germans. Were not the brutal, callous Prussians anyway exclusively responsible for all the disagreeable phenomena of German history?

In this remarkable post-war atmosphere of reconstruction, one should not forget the role played by the Austrian woman. She had a vital part in softening up the rank and file of the occupying forces; many regiments suffered casualties far greater than those inflicted on them by the German Wehrmacht. The entire attitude was summed up perfectly by Dornford Yates in his post-war bestseller *Cost Price* (London, 1949):

'Good afternoon, Madam,' says Mansel, raising his hat.

'Surely it is not your duty to iron the shirt of the Boche.'

'No, sir,' said the woman. 'It isn't. But what can I do? When my husband was ordered to lodge him, the servants left. And so I must wait upon his highness, lest worse befall. I must prepare his breakfast and take it up to his room. Our salon is at his disposal; our bedroom is his. He never opens his mouth, except to complain or to threaten. I have, sir, to clean his shoes – and I am an Austrian woman, the wife of an Austrian lawyer and the daughter of an Austrian judge.'

'Madam,' said Mansel, 'you have my sympathy. My friend and I are English –'

'Alas, sir, we fought against you.'

'Against your will. We know that it was the Boche that forced your hand. England and Austria were always friends.'

Suddenly, to be Austrian rather than German was obviously right. Among those who welcomed the Austrian flag no doubt there were opportunists who secretly regretted the passing of the Reich, but many more had had their traditional prejudices against the Germans all too easily confirmed by the events of the previous seven years. The Austrians had learnt the hard way that they were very different from the Germans.

Just how difficult it was for the Austrians to come to this conclusion is illustrated by the remarkable story of the Austrian Vice-Chancellor of post-war years, Adolf Scharf. Scharf relates how the idea of an independent Austria flashed across his mind one day in 1943 and that from that moment onwards he fought to secure his ideal, which now seemed 'so obvious and clear'. That he remained so hazy about this ideal up to 1943 is less the result of any opportunism than of the sheer implausibility of an independent Austria of just over seven million. This gradual awareness rapidly became widespread and doubtless eased the transition to peace.

As early as 27 April 1945 a provisional Austrian government was able to form under Soviet aegis in Vienna. This included the socialist Karl Renner, who became the new Chancellor even though he, like many other Austrians, had welcomed the Anschluss and had thus survived the last seven years unharmed. Also present were the former Christian socialist Leopold Figl, who had spent most of the seven years in concentration camps, and prewar communist refugees like Johann Koplenig and Ernst Fischer, who were brought back from Moscow in Soviet planes.

Austria had been partitioned into four administrative zones by the Allies. Vienna too was made up of various zones, and the all-important first district was patrolled by all the powers. The devastation of the city and the problems of the joint administration of the first district were brought to the attention of a wide audience in the early fifties by Carol Reed's film *The Third Man*.

Strict rationing and the requisitioning of private property and major hotels by the occupying military gave the Austrians an unpleasant taste of the fruits of the vanquished. Those living in eastern Austria also had to contend with the probability that the Soviet troops who had looted and destroyed their way across the country were there to stay. More than one Austrian believed Austria would never be able to reconstitute itself. Several emigrated, and as the democratic governments of Eastern Europe collapsed like a pack of cards across Stalin's table, there seemed increasingly little likelihood that Austria would be exempt from the Kremlin's *realpolitik* and would be rid of the Soviets. Partly because of the atrocities of Soviet soldiery – discipline tended to be weakest in this army when it came to relations with the civilian population – the Communist Party suffered a dramatic drop in popularity.

The first noteworthy feature about the polls held in Austria in November 1945 was the communist fiasco. They won only four out of 165 seats in the new parliament. Such was the effect of the Russian cavalry turning Viennese cafés into stables and the Russian soldier dealing justice at every corner to the capitalist Austrians. They had to be wealthy capitalists – they had cotton pillows and mechanical lavatories. Those who were truly well off were treated with even less respect, as was shown by what happened in the older estates of the country. Near Hollabrunn one family's medieval castle was partly destroyed, its priceless collection of books and minerals transported back to Moscow and Leningrad and its ballroom converted into a parking area for tanks. Any oil-painting depicting an Austrian officer was desecrated with knives or bayonets or shot to ribbons.

The extent of this vandalism has never been forgotten by the Austrians, and it provided a powerful impetus for their desire to be reincorporated into the Western order of things after the war. The Western Allies recognized this.

They also realized that with a country as close to demoralization as Austria was, there was no question of saddling the country with the kind of war guilt denazification programmes in Germany were producing.

Austria would have to be, if not a bulwark against the East, at least a neutral barrier to prevent communism from seizing the heart of Europe. But neutrality requires independence, and independence requires confidence, and for the Austrians to regain that, the traumatic events of the last seven years would have to be put behind them. To encourage Austrian nationalism the Allies promoted the political parties, who were encouraged to soften their traditional, pre-war fanaticism. In many cases this was happening anyway. Shared experiences in concentration camps, for example, helped lead the many different factions of the conservative People's Party to sink their differences. A note of consensus was struck which to this day sets the tone of Austrian politics.

As well as the beleaguered Communist Party, three major parties emerged to carry the torch of Austrian democracy into the future. The People's Party represented the Catholic provinces and the middle-to-right wing of political thinking; the socialists, building on their admirable record of inter-war development, spoke for those on the Left; in 1949 a third force appeared, which was renamed the Freedom Party in 1955. This party, though it was never to monopolize power, came to be the party which best expressed the paradoxes of Austrian political life. Designed to safeguard the individual from the tyranny of the Right and the collectivism of the Left, it became a rallying point for Austria's pan-Germans. In many cases such people had difficulties joining any of the other parties. Among its earliest recruits were the pre-war Nazi Minister of Agriculture Rheinthaler, and a German-born ex-colonel called Stendebach. Its leaders' antics never posed any serious threat to the stability which the coalition government of the two major parties achieved for Austria, but the party survived. Its meteoric rise to fame in the 1980s, however, could not have been foreseen then.

There was much which could not have been foreseen in the fifties. At the beginning of the decade there can be no doubt that, however responsible Austria's politicians, few people imagined that independence and an end to four-power occupation might be just round the corner. But as the cold war developed, safeguarding Austria's freedom by a state treaty became an important card for both the West and the East.

On 8 February 1955 Mr Molotov announced in a speech to the Supreme Soviet that the Russians would evacuate Austria, provided the four powers guaranteed to 'prevent any future Anschluss between Austria and Germany'. The Soviets, who had for so long dragged their heels over Austria, now seemed eager to show their amiability towards the country in a new propaganda drive. Certainly 1955 was a year conducive to such magnanimity. There can be little doubt that the following year's events in Hungary would have put Austria's independence on ice for some time to come. Austria, however, was spared such a fate as the Soviets rushed to complete Austria's treaty by May.

On 15 May the Austrian Chancellor waved to a jubilant crowd a piece of paper securing his country's independence. The Second Republic was born.

In domestic politics the immediate effect of this was to strengthen the Austrian spirit of consensus. In terms of foreign policy, an offensive began which was to prove remarkably successful in re-establishing Austria's traditional role as a bridge between East and West. One Austrian politician stands above all others as the supreme architect of this development: Bruno Kreisky.

Until his resignation in 1983, Kreisky powerfully reinforced the belief that Austria deserved a place on the international stage. His distinctions lay in many directions, but even his enemies, of which there were certainly many, would admit that in the important sphere of oratory he was unrivalled. To listen to Dr Kreisky lambast his opponents in parliament with a voice whose nasal twang has become almost extinct in Vienna was a unique experience.

Kreisky was representative of two sections of pre-war Austrian society which no longer exist in any significant numbers. First, he was a Jew and secondly, he was a member of the old Jewish bourgeoisie which made up so much of Vienna's middle class in the last century. He wore well-tailored pin-striped suits, and his manner was always that of the hectoring man of affairs rather than the leader of a party whose support was largely to be found in the factories of the country. That he was clever, the Austrians conceded. That, thanks to his high profile abroad and his role as a mediator in international affairs, Vienna had become the European headquarters of the

Organization of Petroleum Exporting Countries, the International Atomic Energy Agency and other prestigious groups, could not be denied.

As more and more capital poured into the country from these bodies and Viennese rents rocketed as demand outstripped supply, Kreisky pursued a policy of extravagant welfare state socialism. Vivid memories of the hardships of Austria before the war were partly responsible for this. 'We know all too well what happens if there is unemployment in Austria,' Kreisky was fond of saying. In order to prevent such a recurrence, a policy of unprecedented subsidy and job security was pursued. Bureaucrats proliferated. As in the days of the Habsburg empire, regular hours, high rates of pay and particularly generous pensions were the most important things in most Austrians' lives. Austrians again fell into their happiest state – they were being administered rather than governed.

In the atmosphere of unreality which lies so heavily about Vienna, the fruits of this policy were quickly to be seen. *Beamte*, or bureaucrats, 'organized' a vast machine of state intervention. Such bureaucracies feed on inertia and cloak responsibility. They destroy ambition and individual initiative. Most of the young Austrians with any drive soon left the country, and the upper echelons of management in West Germany show how successful they were in a climate which favours enterprise.

Thanks to the agreement between managers and trade unionists, social or industrial strife was unheard of. Time lost through strikes in the country could be measured in minutes a year, or even seconds. The state administered industry with a paternal benevolence worthy of the imperial crown. A railway man was well paid, could apply for early retirement and was able each year to travel first class with his family throughout the country at no expense to anyone but the tax payer. Such privileges still exist in most of the country's industries. Indeed, privilege is a key word in this kind of society, for with taxes high and regulations stifling in their complexity, the perk takes on a new and powerful significance. As inflation was low and there was never the slightest hint of economic instability, this regime was allowed to flourish. Austrians who marry still receive large sums from the state. For every child born the state pays a monthly sum which dwarfs the paltry amounts Britain's welfare state hands out. Largess seemed to be the hallmark of these measures, which cushioned the young as well as the old. In Vienna and Graz and Salzburg the universities are flooded with students who see further education as a welcome continuation of school, which need not end until well into their late twenties. For many others it continues until the age of forty and beyond.

Opposition to such policies found little support; even with the recession of the late seventies, few Austrians could plausibly claim their country was in a bad way. Voices might be heard saying that Vienna's underground railway was an extravagance for a city with an already unrivalled system of public transport. Members of the People's Party might occasionally mutter that one day

Austria would have to pay for its generous pensions. Such sirens could be, and have been, largely ignored.

Moreover, with Eastern Europe on the doorstep, it was all too easy to wallow in self-congratulatory excess. Though Austria rightly deserves praise for the role she has played in allowing refugees from all the Eastern European countries to cross her frontiers, most Austrians have little time for such people; and if they address themselves to their Eastern neighbours, it is to remind them that they were very foolish to cast off their links with the empire. *Schadenfreude* was certainly evident among the Austrians when the Russians sent their tanks into Budapest, while in 1968 the fate of the Czechs, a race traditionally despised by the Austrians, provoked a similar, curious mixture of pity and pleasure.

At this time Dr Waldheim, after a career of studied dullness in the ranks of the Austrian foreign service, was Austria's Foreign Minister. His behaviour then has long been a source of some controversy, for those who were serving in the Austrian Embassy in Prague recall all too well how they received a message from the Foreign Ministry demanding that the issue of visas to Czechs wishing to flee the imminent invasion be halted. They contradict Waldheim's later denial that this was his personal decision. Whether it was Dr Waldheim's own decision or not, its blatant lack of humanity must be attributable in some way to the minister responsible. For some Czechs who managed to get out, the order was mercifully ignored by the Ambassador.

On the domestic front such actions spread few ripples.

Glee that these things could not happen in Austria soon became complacency. Thanks to the presence of international organizations, Austria was always a safe haven. As a result of its tourism and the charms of the Austrian Alps, the country was wealthy and free to regard the prosaic detail of its strategic vulnerability with detachment. Nothing manifested this more than the Austrians' attitude to their defence. Though supposedly based on the Swiss model, it in fact falls very far short of Switzerland's exemplary armed neutrality. Despite the recent purchase of Draken jets from Sweden to replace obsolete Saab aircraft of the fifties, defence continues to be the lowest of the country's priorities. The Austrians still rely on a handful of outdated jets to patrol their airspace. Unlike Switzerland, whose army is taken seriously and is regularly drilled, Austria has no long tradition of neutrality.

The well-equipped Swiss believe they can turn the entire population into an army which would defy any aggressor for months, while the Austrians acknowledge the indefensibility of their eastern frontier and think in terms of stopping an invader for a 'day or two'. Given that Austria has one of the richest military traditions in the world, this attitude is puzzling. It cannot entirely be explained away by geography or the limitations of a small nation. An army which once had the finest uniforms in Europe is now the worst dressed and equipped. Although it proved its courage time and again on the battlefields of Europe and was the first to defeat Napoleon on land, today it does not possess a single bayonet, even for ceremonial purposes. This may at first seem somewhat irrelevant to modern Austria's difficulties, but on closer examination there can be no doubt that the Austrian army expresses perfectly the problem the country has with its past.

Years of socialist administration have distanced people's minds from its less socialist history. The Habsburgs are sufficiently remote and the present Austrian aristocracy so excessively enfeebled as to permit nostalgia for distant, imperial days. More recent events are submerged and simply not addressed; this is true of the Nazi period and of such Catholic Austrian politicians of the thirties as Dollfuss. It is ironic that the one Austrian politician who gave his life defying the Nazis is not commemorated either by a monument or by a prominent square in any of Austria's cities. It is equally ironic that the Austrian army, with its centuries of tradition, is organized along most untraditional lines.

In this no man's land of blind areas and unreality, it is perhaps only to be expected that the Austrian soldier has to grope for some imagery of the past. Soldiers, perhaps more than the members of any other profession, like to feel part of a long-established concern, and they work all the better when they have that feeling. The preservation of tradition, therefore, even if it is only in some minor item of dress, is usually an important matter. Not, however, in the Second Republic. In the vacuum created by a policy whose aim is the banishing of tradition, the modern Austrian soldier finds only a regrettable fascination for the days of the Third Reich. 'It was, after all, arguably the most successful army of the twentieth century,' one eager corporal explains.

When a subject is not discussed, criticism is all the more difficult and a balanced evaluation of ideas impossible. In this way, the lack of confidence in the imperial or Catholic tradition, which has every right to call itself as patriotic as Austrian socialism, has created among Austrians of all professions a myopic view of history. It should also be said that the Allies must share some responsibility for encouraging the Austrians to turn a blind eye to their recent history.

No Austrian school teaches its pupils that what Dollfuss did for Austria was to his credit or that the Second World War was a very different affair from any other war. Quite intelligent children and, indeed, students in their late teens will make the statement that, as far as they can see, Hitler was 'just like Napoleon'.

Thus, while on the one hand Kreisky gave the Austrians a voice in international affairs and an important role to play in Europe, coupled with a degree of comfort those who had experienced pre-war Austria would never have thought possible, it was achieved at the expense of any serious appraisal of Austria's role in events earlier this century. This may seem only a minor defect, but it has cost Austria dearly.

Before 1955 Allied military instructions required that all German Wehrmacht personnel be officially discharged by Allied authorities. Oberleutnant Waldheim was forced to join other soldiers in Schladming on 18 May 1945 and was subsequently transported in a truck column to a US detention camp in Bavaria. In June 1945, after preliminary screening, he was released but, before taking up a post with the Austrian foreign service, Waldheim had already become a file on what was to be established as the United Nations War Crimes Commission.

Case number R/N/684 accused Oberleutnant Waldheim of being responsible for 'retaliation actions carried out by the Wehrmacht units in Yugoslavia, inasmuch as the "Heeresgruppe E" was involved in directing the retaliation orders issued by the OKW [*Oberkommando der Wehrmacht*]. Thus the Ic staff of the "Heeresgruppe E" were the means for the massacre of numerous sections of the Serb population' (see Appendix, Document 1).

Though the Commission's committee I, which last met in 1948, was convinced of a prima-facie case against Waldheim, it was not judicially empowered to do anything about this. The larger fish, such as Kaltenbrunner, Seyss-Inquart and eventually Eichmann were run to ground and brought to justice at Nuremberg and elsewhere, but the infrastructure of the Nazi machine posed enormous problems for such a commission. Add to this the pro-Austrian atmosphere encountered at the end of the war and it is easy to see how, without conclusive evidence, Waldheim, like many others, was not subjected to too arduous an ordeal. Growing distrust of the Yugoslavs, especially after their barbaric massacring of repatriated Croats, Serbs and Slovenes in 1945, also probably contributed to a slackening of the hunt for those who may have carried out orders involving atrocities in the Balkans.

By 1947 the Austrians themselves were launching their own offensive against too much denazification with the celebrated, if rather embarrassing, series of 'Red–White–

Red' books, which attempted to present some of the facts about the Austrian resistance. The effect of such efforts tends to be diametrically opposed to the one desired, as was the case with the no less inadequate 'White Book', issued to defend Waldheim thirty years later. Nevertheless, the 'Red–White–Red' series was another indication of the way the wind was blowing. It could afford to remain incomplete because of the Allies' reluctance to prosecute its cases and to shatter a small nation's precious morale by conducting uninterrupted hunts for Nazis. Visits from the authorities, who asked awkward questions about details of wartime careers, began to become less frequent. Such actions, however, created a country which inevitably would one day be vulnerable. As Austria grew prosperous, this vulnerability might be overlooked. With a gifted Jewish Chancellor at the helm, no one was going to accuse the country of harbouring either serious neo-Nazi tendencies or rampant anti-Semitism. In the same way, no one could exploit Austria's lack of any sense of history and stir up nostalgia for the Third Reich. Accusations in 1983 that the Freedom Party MP Herr Friedrich Peter had been involved with the SS in atrocities during the war quickly blew over, damaging Herr Peter's political ambitions but leaving the fabric of the country untouched. It was known that there were a few Nazis in Austria, but this was no reason for the country to be ostracized or condemned.

In 1983 an event took place which was to have far-reaching consequences for Austria. At the general election of that year the socialists failed to hold on to their absolute majority. Kreisky, by now an old and far from well man, decided to resign. It was without doubt the end of an era, but there was no reason why Austria should not continue to enjoy the goodwill of the international community. Consensus politics meant that there would be few social or economic issues which would arouse any passions. If anything, the country would become quieter and less controversial after the retirement of its high-profile Chancellor.

Moreover, Kreisky had formulated a strategy for his country's future and had planned Austria's post-Kreisky era carefully. A small coalition between the socialists and the Freedom Party would preserve Austria's socialist policies and deprive the conservative People's Party of power for another ten years. The right-wing Freedom Party was sufficiently on the fringe of politics to be little more than a passenger on what would still be a predominantly socialist ship. Austria would remain the 'island of happy souls', the envy of socialist politicians throughout Europe and the stable rock at the heart of the continent.

That within three years Kreisky's life-work would be in ruins and that Austria would be the subject of bitter attacks and shunned was not to be foreseen; but then, even the best-laid plans depend on luck and skill. These two qualities were to prove woefully short in supply during the next few years.

CHAPTER FOUR

CRACKS IN THE FAÇADE

From the beginning the new coalition government marked a change of style. The policies might be similar and the social consensus might still be the lynchpin of the country's political well-being, but the new Chancellor, Dr Fred Sinowatz, was a man in an entirely different mould from that of his predecessor. A native of Burgenland, Austria's most backward and impoverished province, Dr Sinowatz's appearance showed all the traces of the Hungarian and gypsy blood which runs through the veins of the inhabitants of this easternmost *Bundesland*.

A figure who very much seemed a man of the soil as well as of the people, Dr Sinowatz was the first to admit that his looks were in sharp contrast to those of his elegant predecessor. 'With a face like mine, I never imagined I should have much of a future in politics,' he candidly told West German television following his arrival at the Ballhausplatz Chancellery. Often to be seen eating ham and eggs at the nearby Café Landtmann, Dr Sinowatz's easy manner was less popular with the Austrians than it was among members of the foreign press, who enjoyed such accessibility.

Intellectuals who were not socialists dubbed him the Burgenland Marxist. Less intellectual Austrians moaned daily about the Chancellor's appalling appearance and dress sense and how scandalous this was for the country. In the prosperous west of the country, around Salzburg, the Tyrol and Vorarlberg, the new Chancellor personified the Balkanization of Austria. His appointment appeared to mark the triumph of Eastern values over Western. This was borne out by neighbouring Bavaria, where stickers were printed asking, 'Who the hell is Sinowatz?'

In later months, when Dr Waldheim's own campaign was fully under way, such superficial judgements on appearance were to play an important role. Had Austria been ruled by a Chancellor who cut a smarter figure, I have little doubt that support for Waldheim would not have been as great. In a small country whose election campaigns are largely fought on the nation's billboards, which are smothered with countless copies of the candidates' photographs, such things take on an unnaturally powerful significance.

Austrians who had groaned and whinged under Kreisky's leadership now found themselves regarding their former Chancellor with nostalgic longing. It did not impress them that Sinowatz understood brilliantly the Austrian mind. His fascination for the baroque (on which he had written his doctoral thesis), his love of improvisation, his intimate sense of the grotesque – these were all lost on the majority of Austrians, who, regardless of the man's ability, were obsessed with visual effect. In the *trompe-l'oeil* world of Austrian politics, Sinowatz was an unfortunate putto replacing the once dazzling prince.

The new Chancellor's coalition partners also offered little inspiration for most Austrians. The Freedom Party had in their leader, Herr Norbert Steger, a young politician of extravagant mediocrity. Herr Steger's only redeeming quality was that in a party which harboured many pan-German nationalists, he was a figure of the Left. He was therefore out of tune with his own party and always vulnerable, but at the same time he was an ideal companion for Dr Sinowatz. Unfortunately, such advantages cut little ice with the Austrians, who were horrified by some of the antics of the Vice-Chancellor. At newspaper interviews he did not know the meaning of *détente*. In public speeches he often contradicted the government's agreed policies or even missed the point of what he should be talking about. The former Vienna choirboy, with his comic moustache, moaning voice and general air of lassitude, drifted around the imposing former Ministry of War on the Ringstrasse like a ghostly puppet searching for those things which elude most Austrians: understanding and simplicity.

Steger's manner was compounded by a factor which, if of no relevance in any other country, was to count against him in Austria. One bright morning Dr Steger appeared at the baroque Press Club in the Bankgasse, a biscuit's throw away from the Burgtheater, Vienna's principal shrine to Austrian drama. The events which followed what was to be a routine press conference almost suggested that the Vice-Chancellor had lost his way. Theatre, never a rare aspect of Austrian life, suddenly became the only suitable description for what ensued.

An Austrian journalist, who was certainly no friend of the Freedom Party, asked Steger if it were true that one of his parents had been of Jewish origin. This astonishing and irrelevant question met with an even more astonishing reply. Fighting back tears, the Vice-Chancellor sobbed in front of a packed room of journalists that yes, it was true, he possessed Jewish blood. That Herr Steger should feel so embarrassed and emotional about this is difficult to imagine, but it was a fact which had been suppressed and he was all too aware of how anti-Semitic Austrians could be. His party too would be unwilling to allow it to pass without negative comment. All political parties depend on support from factions which are often close to the certifiable, and for the nationalist pan-German supporters of the Freedom Party, the reason for Herr Steger's lack of charisma was now blatantly obvious. He was not even *reindeutsch* (pure German).

A few months before this unpleasant incident, Professor Weiss of the University of Vienna had published a study on anti-Semitism in Austria, in which she concluded that nearly a quarter of all Austrians were 'virulently anti-Semitic'. Based on questionnaires answered over a period of time, Professor Weiss had found traces of anti-Semitism among the young, as well as among older Austrians. What was so remarkable about this study was that it highlighted the survival of hostility in a time when hardly any Jews were left in the country. Again and again the Professor was confronted with Austrians who believed that the Jews had too great an influence among financiers and the press. Despite there being fewer than 10,000 Jews in modern Austria, the modern Austrian believed the Jews were behind every significant financial move.

Many writers in the earlier part of this century commented on the remarkable strength of anti-Jewish feeling in Vienna. Long before Hitler forced the Jews into camps and to wear the yellow star, Jews were limited to ghettos by imperial Habsburg decree. In the late nineteenth century, though given considerable freedom in Vienna, Jews were often the victims of discrimination and even violence. The cry '*Raus mit den Juden*' was heard – and still is heard – with alarming frequency. In those days almost a quarter of the population of Vienna was Jewish, and the Austrians, prone to paranoia, felt threatened by their presence, energy and talents.

Partly because the denazification of Austria was so half-hearted and partly because Austrians were allowed to enter the post-war world as victims of Nazism, a dangerous illusion was allowed to flourish. Today Austrians young and old may be heard to say that only a fraction of the number of Jews 'supposed to have died' in the war were killed by the Nazis and that after the war all the Jews were generously compensated for their 'hardships'. 'They got everything back.' 'They stick together. Of course, nothing like as many as six million Jews were gassed during the war – worse luck.' So went the chit-chat of one Austrian I encountered ten years ago in Graz and such is the language of many younger Austrians in Vienna.

When Steger was asked about his 'racial origins', the journalist was posing a question reminiscent of those asked by the Gestapo agent, and a seemingly harmless detail of family history was elevated to nightmarish trauma. At first the incident so embarrassed most of those present that there was virtually a news black-out on the press conference. But eventually the news got out, and within the week cartoons of Herr Steger in orthodox Jewish dress were to be seen in the extreme right-wing publications of his own party. Among most Austrians, although another black mark could now be chalked up against the Vice-Chancellor and the government, there was as yet no hint of any deeper backlash of anti-Jewish hostility. For a brief period the higher standards of the earlier Kreisky era prevailed. Not, however, for very long.

One of the more noteworthy features of the junior coalition party in the government was that the ministers were all young. Steger was still in his thirties, while another young man, Friedhelm Frischenschlager, was in charge at the Ministry of Defence. As young men they were clearly not in any way tainted by the war generation of their party. They could plausibly claim to be the new shining image of the party. With such men at the helm, the gibe that the Freedom Party only consisted of 'old Nazis' sounded a little thin.

Frischenschlager, however, seemed a little too fond of attending reunions of S S veterans in the notoriously right-wing province of Salzburg to be entirely on the side of the angels. Such doubts were initially dispelled by his appearance at the former Nazi concentration camp of Mauthausen on the Danube, where he gave a stirring speech, urging that no one should ever forget the dreadful events which took place in the camp during the war. For the first time in Austria's history the passing-out parade of army recruits took place at Mauthausen. Frischenschlager said:

> Normally such a parade would be a notable ceremony, held to the applause of all present, but not at such a terrible place as this. I wanted to have the parade here to remind our young people of the democratic values which we hold to be so important and for which so many people suffered and died here at Mauthausen . . . People are still suffering and dying elsewhere in the world in defence of those same basic freedoms.

It was an encouraging gesture. Throughout the world the new minister was seen to represent the Austria Kreisky had spent his lifetime constructing: mature, with a realistic view of the past. Unfortunately, experience was not on the minister's side when it came to the first challenge of his career a month or so later

January 1985 was particularly cold. As usual, it was the height of the ball season, and Vienna, like every other city in the country, was dancing its evenings away, oblivious to external events and, indeed, to anything but trivia. Perhaps because the city was in something of a stupor, the news that a former Austrian war criminal, the S S officer Walter Reder, would be repatriated to Austria was treated with little more than a yawn. On the eve of the prestigious 'Theresianistin picnic', held in the Haus der Industriellen Vereinigung, an Italian military aircraft made its way across the Alps to deposit the former Obersturmbannführer safely at Graz.

If the Austrians were largely oblivious to such events, so too were the members of the World Jewish Congress, who had decided to hold their annual meeting in Vienna for the first time. This decision more than any other illustrated the full extent of the international Jewish community's confidence in Austria. Many of the delegates had lost relations in the Holocaust, and more than a few of them had been born in the old crown lands of the Austrian empire. Vienna was thus a city of nostalgia but also of bitterness for them, and their meeting in the Austrian capital took on a particular significance.

Such symbolism was largely lost on the young Herr Frischenschlager, who proceeded to greet Reder personally on his arrival at Graz airport. Such an act was indefensible. After the war Reder had been tried and found guilty of serious war crimes by an Italian court. He had ordered the execution of 1,830 Italian civilians in the area of Marzabotto. The hated murderer of Marzabotto, as he was named by the Italians, had been sentenced to life imprisonment, but as an act of mercy the Italian government had agreed to release the sick, old man so that he could be repatriated to Austria.

An act of mercy on the part of Reder's victims was transformed into a crass act of defiance thanks to Frischenschlager, who not only shook hands with Reder on his arrival, but also accompanied him in an Austrian military aircraft to the military hospital of Baden, near Vienna. When word of this leaked out – as it had to in a city like Vienna – there was immediate outrage. The World Jewish Congress broke up in dismay, and not even the personal intervention of Chancellor Sinowatz could prevent the delegates from leaving the city in protest. From all over the world telegrams demanding the minister's resignation poured in, and the Socialist Party rapidly distanced itself from the minister's action. It was a political error, the socialists said, and Frischenschlager, stunned by the reaction, conceded, 'Yes, I admit I made a mistake.'

It is possible that far from meeting Reder with the deliberate intention of rallying Nazi supporters in his party, Frischenschlager behaved with more naïvety than calculation. He honestly had no idea that what he was doing was wrong. For this perverse way of thinking the events of Austria's first post-war years are as much to blame as anything. The fact that the Austrian press largely supported the minister revealed immediately how widespread such illusions were and how lamentably Austrians had failed to educate a younger generation about the complexities of their country's past. Frischenschlager at a stroke destroyed in minutes the work of years and revealed to the whole world his countryman's lack of historical perspective. After achieving this he flew off to Cairo for an official visit to Egypt. Within hours, however, he was recalled to face the gathering fire of indignation. He was ill-prepared.

Equally revealing of his myopic view of his behaviour were the minister's panicky statements explaining his actions. If the Austrians' proneness to show a lack of moral fibre in a crisis needed more dramatic expression, it would have been difficult to find a more vivid example. Like a child stumbling and stuttering in front of a glowering headmaster, Frischenschlager made one absurd statement after another. 'I was there purely in my personal capacity . . .' 'I should never have done it if I had thought someone was going to find out . . .' 'It was a great mistake.' Wobbly words, which were to be echoed less than two years later by another Austrian politician, equally amazed by the furore surrounding his actions.

The words failed to impress those bodies in Austrian society which retained some perspective of the past. Among these, the army proved surprisingly resilient. The former chief of the Austrian General Staff, General Emil Spannochi, denounced Frischenschlager as a 'stain on the honour of the Austrian army'. Like most institutions in Austria, the army is divided on a party basis. Over the years many officers have noted with dismay the nostalgia for an army which fought with the Nazis, but enough officers remain who are prepared to distance themselves from the German Wehrmacht. These Austrians were horrified by an action which strongly implied a link between the present Austrian army and the wartime SS. Another officer, Colonel Karl Semlitsch, said it was 'infamous' to refer to Reder as a 'former Austrian major'. As the number of voices clamouring for the minister's resignation grew, only one politician insisted that Frischenschlager had done the right thing. In Carinthia, a notoriously pan-German province with many former Nazis, the local leader of the Freedom Party, Herr Jörg Haider, called Reder a 'German soldier who had done his duty'.

Haider, who was to rise to spectacular heights in Austrian politics, had already carved a reputation for himself in Carinthia by pledging to end bilingual teaching in

Carinthian schools, where some of the children are Slovene. This would have driven the Slovenes into a ghetto, making them even more insecure and despised, but it was a popular move with the people in Carinthia, who were afraid of being undermined by Slavs, and it brought the charismatic Herr Haider many votes. A group of his supporters even went so far as to organize a list of possible employers for Reder on his release from hospital.

Although the leader of the party, Herr Steger, distanced himself from Haider's remarks, there was no doubt about what was happening, not only in the Freedom Party but in Austria as a whole. As the Western press criticized the Austrians, a closing of ranks was perceptible; in places it became tinged with anti-Semitic remarks. 'Of course the press is against us – it's dominated by Jews,' I was told one morning at breakfast shortly afterwards by a young veterinary student. 'Frischenschlager made a mistake, but it's not worth resigning over. He's young; he'll learn.' Foreign observers were less impressed.

Despite the pressure to resign from abroad, after a three-hour meeting of the cabinet Frischenschlager was able to retain his post. A vote of no confidence in the government failed and the storm was weathered, thanks to the strict party discipline which dominates Austrian politics and overrules any Western concepts of ministerial responsibility. The party had given Frischenschlager his position; only the party could take it away from him. Thus, though the young minister had brought dishonour to his country and to his government, he was able to survive on account of his party's fears of annoying the pan-German neo-Nazi vote which makes up so much of its support.

The affair blew over by the spring, but a number of hard lessons had been given, if not learnt. The first of these was that Austria was a very vulnerable country in terms of its image abroad. For years an effusively charming Austrian diplomatic service had succeeded, with the help of music and *Kunst*, in persuading the world that Hitler had been a German and Beethoven an Austrian. Suddenly all this was in ruins.

Secondly, the Austrians had insulted and injured the powerful World Jewish Congress. Jews everywhere realized that any truce between the West and Kreisky's Austria was a thing of the past. Austria was now open season.

Thirdly, and for the Austrians this was the most significant point, a disagreeable reminder of the country's ambivalent role during the Second World War had had to be faced. When the crisis came, it was handled with a mixture of incompetence and feebleness. It was an unpleasant augury of things to come. Wiser men were by no means exaggerating when they said that such an event would never have been possible under Kreisky.

Fourthly, anti-Semitism and neo-Nazi feelings had again come to the surface in Austrian politics. The passions Reder aroused in the West and in Jewish communities was matched by a revaluation of his role by many right-wing Austrians.

If Frischenschlager had won support among the brown fringes of his party, he soon lost it by his apologies, especially the formal one to Israel, which was greeted with particular hostility. When it was published in the Israeli paper *Yediot Aharonot*, Frischenschlager soon found himself taken to task at home for referring to Reder as a war criminal rather than as a prisoner of war. Haider described the minister's words to the Israelis as 'an unnecessary explanation'. Reder, said Haider, using words which were to become all too familiar a year or two later, had 'only done his duty'. More ominously, the Carinthian leader said he would call for a special meeting of the party's Executive Committee to discuss the apology. The strident note from the provinces was becoming louder. The situation calmed down once again, but it was becoming increasingly clear to the government that their credit with the Austrian electorate was rapidly running out. For the socialists the right-wing Freedom Party was becoming a liability.

New heights of absurdity and incompetence were reached a few months later with the revelations of the celebrated wine scandal. As it was a quiet summer and little was happening, the world's media, alerted because of Frischenschlager to the presence of copy in Austria, swooped. The scandal was a typically Austrian affair. Far from being the work of one mastermind, it was caused by a series of corrupt growers and dealers who poisoned virtually everything they could get their hands on. They had done such things for years with impunity; adulterating fruit juices, making red wine from grape refuse and chemically strengthening certain *Auslese* vintages. Like Frischenschlager's naïve defence of his behaviour towards

Reder, the average defence of the wine adulterers focused on their belief that they were not doing anything really dishonest or immoral.

The ease with which Austrians tolerate corruption owes much to their geography. It was Metternich who said the Orient begins on the Landstrasse, and he was intelligent enough to realize that this was a question of mentality as much as geography. When confronted with repression, the flexibility of the Balkan mind can soon generate a lack of fibre and a fear of independent thinking. At Austrian universities and schools, for example, cheating at exams carries none of the stigma it has in other countries. For graduates and school-leavers the all-important word is 'protection'. This means knowing someone who will do you a favour, in return for which you may be called upon to help out at some stage. It is an order of things which thrives on the easygoing Viennese character and is naturally something which does not encourage merit or moral responsibility. Combine this with naïvety and a false perspective of history, and it is perhaps not surprising that the Austrians behave the way they do and that Frischenschlager felt he had been victimized for his actions.

Any sign, however, that the young minister was chastened by his experience or that he had been able to broaden his historical perspectives through his ordeal by fire was slow in forthcoming. In fact, the experience seemed to make him even more uncertain. A year later he tacitly condoned the erection in the military academy of Wiener Neustadt of a plaque commemorating a Nazi war criminal. It may be recalled that Waldheim had served in the Balkans under a General Alexander Löhr, commander of Army Group E. It was this unit which had committed reprisals against civilians up and down the peninsula. Löhr was an Austrian, and in the First World War he had distinguished himself as a pilot in the Austrian air force and had helped re-establish it in the post-Habsburg world of the 1920s. Tried by a Yugoslav military court after the war, Löhr was sentenced to death and shot on 26 February 1947. As well as commanding Army Group E, Löhr had masterminded the bombing of Belgrade, in which 17,000 lives were lost, most of them civilians.

Despite his execution for war crimes, several officers attached to the military academy considered a memorial plaque in honour of Löhr suitable. The plaque said that Löhr was the commandant and creator of the Austrian air force. It made no mention of the manner of his death. A stiffly worded protest from Belgrade and criticism from several Austrian officers resulted in the removal of the plaque, but the hapless Herr Frischenschlager came out of the affair rather badly. Herr Übeleis, Minister for Construction, ordered that the plaque, which Frischenschlager had allowed to be erected, be taken down. It was said he was the minister responsible for such things; Herr Frischenschlager had not been aware of its presence, the official communiqués ran.

Once again the unhappy association with the German Wehrmacht had been allowed to come to the fore. Once again the responsible minister had failed to honour his calling. And, of course, once again the brilliant opportunist Herr Haider was able to rush in and express the feelings of the neo-Nazi minority. The plaque, he said, had been removed because communists and left-wing groups had forced the Austrian government to neglect its history. The 'apotheosis of unreality' was at work again.

As the year ended more scandals came to light to give the impression of a *Skandalrepublik*. An abbot was found to be womanizing and hoarding thousands of pounds; the Foreign Minister was called as a witness at an important fraud trial. Socialism without a charismatic leader was proving extremely dubious, and the following year there would be presidential and general elections. Whether Austrian socialism would survive in its present form into the new century would be decided in 1986. With little to show for its three years of rule but an ever increasing debt and the ridicule of the world's media, the government could only feel fragile. Attention focused on the forthcoming presidential election. This more than anything would show which way the wind was blowing. A breakthrough by the opposition People's Party could lead to a landslide victory at the autumn general election. For the first time in years a non-socialist party stood a reasonable chance of doing well in a general election.

These circumstances meant that the presidential election, however unpolitical it was supposed to be, would become the strategic key to the two main parties' futures. In Austria the President, as head of state, should be above politics; in the election, however, candidates were to be fielded by the main parties. As a result a contest which should have been based on personality became a party, and thereby political, conflict. The socialists felt that it was essential to win in order to stay on top, while the opposition felt it was vital to win in order to stand any chance of governing the country. Perhaps no presidential election in Austria was to be as important for the future of the country's politics as this one.

The stakes throughout the country were going to be high and risks could be taken, even though the eventual winner would be nothing more than a figure-head. In Austria atmosphere is all, and among the country's politicians there was a feeling that the old impartial regime of President Rudolf Kirchschläger might not be echoed by his successor. In terms of patronage, if not constitutional power, the President was a vital card. With such a formidable Chancellor as Bruno Kreisky and a strong socialist government, the President's role had been largely insignificant. But with the Sinowatz–Steger circus, this was unlikely to remain the case. Both sides therefore prepared for a titanic struggle.

In fact, neither of the two main candidates was particularly impressive. Dr Kurt Steyrer, the socialist candidate and a former Health Minister, was blessed with a smile which, reproduced on the grotesque scale demanded by Austrian election posters, resembled an advertisement for toothpaste. His rival, Dr Kurt Waldheim, squinting in a sinister way out of frog-like eyes, looked horribly smug. Waldheim was, like Kreisky, an international Austrian, but one that was far from liked. At the Austrian Foreign Ministry, where memories of his tenure were still recalled with a shudder, there was a particular *frisson* of unease.

'Perhaps in a country like ours, an unpopular man, an unintelligent man, a mediocre man can rise to the top,' a veteran conservative journalist confided as the year began. Waldheim seemed, despite all, to be a safe bet.

CHAPTER FIVE

WALDHEIM FOR PRESIDENT

A visitor to Austria always knows when an election is imminent. He or she need not understand a word of German, need have little interest in local politics or, indeed, any interest in Austria – a glimpse at a wall which usually advertises Coca-Cola is enough. Instead of the sophisticated advertisement, a large colour photograph of a candidate inflicts an almost invariably unattractive face on the passer-by. One might expect to find campaigns which deify the ego in a country where selfishness is encountered all too frequently. Policies receive less attention. A politician may be unintelligent and uninspiring, but as long as he *looks* respectable magnified twenty times on a poster, he is acceptable to his party's followers.

Dr Waldheim's problem here was that his appearance, however distinguished, was not in the ski-instructor league; long years of experience have told Austrian campaign managers that such looks win the most votes. His smile was more menacing than avuncular and his countenance evoked a petty arrogance, which usually turns most Austrians off. '*Er sieht aus wie ein Weinkellner*' (He looks like a wine-waiter), observed a Bavarian baroness, perfectly well aware that this type of waiter was to be found in a '*dritte Garnitur*', or third-rate country.

Partly to combat this and partly to capture the

Austrians' longing for an international Austrian, which had been frustrated since Kreisky's departure, it was decided to run Waldheim as 'The man the world trusts'. No doubt this slogan was long pondered and received unanimous approval, but, as is often the case in Austria, it was to have ironic consequences worthy of a Schnitzler comedy. 'You have no idea how difficult it is to sell this man,' one of Waldheim's campaign managers observed, implying that the international slogan was the best he could do. As the posters showing an extremely smug Waldheim against a background of New York skyscrapers went up along the Ringstrasse, the ultimate irony of this approach was invisible to most Austrians. Not, however, to the socialists, who, worried by their own lamentable record and the widespread disenchantment in the country, saw the international dimension as a further threat. If Waldheim was to be discredited, it would have to be internationally. How could that be done? If Herr Frischenschlager had failed to learn any lessons from his roasting the year before, some of the socialists had seen for the first time how crippling the Nazi card could be.

It was known that, like the then President, Rudolf Kirchschläger, Waldheim had served as an officer in the Wehrmacht. While the posters were filling the streets of Vienna, copies of Waldheim's recently published memoirs were filling shop windows. There were some interesting gaps in *In the Eye of the Storm*.

Over a year later an Austrian court was to prove that Austrian journalists' allegations regarding the then Chancellor, Fred Sinowatz, and his Cabinet Secretary,

Hans Pusch, were not libellous. The journalists claimed that the two men had agreed to pass on documents, giving more details of Waldheim's career, to the World Jewish Congress. Dr Sinowatz and his colleagues have always denied that they were engaged in such an underhand move but it is significant that as soon as Waldheim was elected President, Sinowatz resigned.

Certainly, whoever dug around in the archives would tap a rich vein. The question remained, however, as to why no one had done so earlier. Why had Israel, in particular, not found the relevant files? It had every reason to be annoyed with Waldheim, since as UN Secretary-General from 1972 to 1982 he had bent over backwards to defend the Arab's interest. The Mossad, or Israeli security service, was not an organization to pull its punches on such a case.

The revelations which followed over the next few months all suggested a link with the election campaign. Not that such a thought should in any way devalue the allegations which began to dominate the world's headlines. The Austrian weekly magazine *Profil*, the only professional journal in a country whose standards of journalism are lamentably low, published its March issue with a cover story entitled 'Waldheim's Brown Past'. This revealed that Waldheim had been attached to the SA (*Sturmabteilung*), was probably a committed Nazi and had served on the Balkan front. The news fell at first on far from fertile ground; few Western papers took it seriously, and the Austrian attitude was, if true, so what?

A young Dutch woman quoted at the time, who had always worked in journalism and had come from a family which had fought long and hard in the Dutch resistance, thought that the SA connection probably arose because everyone who needed to move officially in military circles at that time had to belong to such an organization. This attitude soon summed up that of most Austrians and was incorporated at an early stage into Waldheim's defence. As the World Jewish Congress in New York flew to the attack, Waldheim appeared on television denying that he had been involved in Nazi atrocities.

In particular, the World Jewish Congress's accusations that he had been involved in the transportation of 42,830 Jews from Salonika to Auschwitz were passionately rejected. But whatever Waldheim said, the allegations began to snowball, and the appearance in *The New York Times* and *The Times* of a photograph showing Waldheim in full Wehrmacht uniform between senior Nazi generals in Montenegro was persuasive. The pose alone seemed to condemn Waldheim as a Nazi who was eager to please his masters. With his back noticeably stiffer than those around him, Waldheim is the perfect example of an Austrian officer who is keen to impress upon his German superiors that he is as reliable as any of his more Teutonic colleagues. It almost looks as if the young Oberleutnant wanted to be part of General Artur Phelps's Seventh SS Volunteer Division instead of just a simple ordnance officer.

The photograph was accompanied by the disclosure that Waldheim, though only a junior officer, had been awarded the order of the Crown of St Zvonimir with silver oak leaves, one of the highest awards of the fascist puppet state of Croatia which had been set up by the Nazis. The presence of the silver oak leaves indicated that it had been earned under fire. Dr Waldheim, who was notoriously covetous of foreign decorations and who had loved collecting them, along with 21-gun salutes, during his tours as UN Secretary-General, must have been particularly irritated that this early example of his passion for bangles had reached the papers.

Suddenly all the posters showing him with the world's leaders, including Mrs Thatcher and President Mitterrand, seemed to be a little off the mark. But if the posters were quickly changed, his party rallied round. Herr Alois Mock, the leader of the conservative People's Party which was supporting him, described the Congress's accusations as a 'monstrosity'. Waldheim himself called them a 'dirty campaign'. Speaking on American television, the former Secretary-General said, 'I do apologize to all my friends in the United States and in Austria that I didn't mention this. If I misled them, I'm sorry . . . it was not my intention to do this.'

But this was as far as atonement went, and for the rest of April 1986 Waldheim and his supporters attacked the World Jewish Congress with acerbic language. The fact that the allegations were now widely seen to be 'Jewish inspired' began to have an effect on the Austrians' attitudes. Almost without exception, the Austrian papers supported the beleaguered candidate. 'Nothing to do with deportations,' screamed the Vienna daily *Kurier*. 'More

Jewish accusations,' echoed the other papers, while across the posters depicting Waldheim appeared the banner with the old Nazi slogan '*Jetzt erst recht*' (Now more than ever), suggesting that on account of the accusations made by the World Jewish Congress, it really *was* right to vote for Waldheim.

This new banner was a particularly ugly development, and Jews in Vienna began to feel the chill. Threatening letters began to pile up at the headquarters of the Jewish Cultural Community in the Seittenstättengasse in the former ghetto of the city, and the slogan '*Juden raus*' was again to be seen daubed on nearby walls. Not surprisingly, Jews in Vienna viewed this with considerable alarm. The fragile tolerance which had marked their stay in Vienna since the war showed every sign of being destroyed. This, too, despite the fact that the city's two most prominent and famous Jews, Bruno Kreisky and Simon Wiesenthal, the celebrated Nazi-hunter, had backed Waldheim's denials.

Wiesenthal's opinion was particularly impressive, though it cut little ice with some members of the World Jewish Congress. Interviewed on British television, Wiesenthal insisted that he had no evidence to suggest that Waldheim could be implicated in war crimes. Nevertheless, Wiesenthal was quick to point out that when Waldheim insisted he did not know about such events, 'He must be mistaken. I do not believe him.'

From the beginning Waldheim's blanket denial of any knowledge of the events in the Balkans seemed very shaky; it sounded like the claim of a panic-stricken man.

Only Herr Johann Auf, a war artist who served with Dr Waldheim in the Balkans, supported his statement that he could have known nothing about the mass transportation of Jews from Salonika to Auschwitz. As the image of an emotional old man being hounded by foreign journalists emerged, Austrians began to feel indignant. Why should they feel guilty anyway? They were not Germans; they were victims of the Nazis. Far from compelling the former UN Secretary-General to heed world opinion and renounce his candidacy, as the World Jewish Congress and the Socialist Party hoped, the allegations and the shaming threat of a boycott by the Western world had apparently rebounded to Waldheim's advantage. This extraordinary circumstance arose because of a number of factors. One was Waldheim's remarkable footwork on the excuses front. For every new allegation there was a new answer, even if it contradicted the old ones.

The first documents provided by the World Jewish Congress presented Waldheim as an intelligence officer, initially based at Salonika, who was a member of two Nazi organizations and who had served for three years in the headquarters of an army group which had ruthlessly murdered thousands of Yugoslavs and had organized the transportation of over 43,000 Greek Jews to Auschwitz. To this Waldheim responded with the defence that as an interpreter he was stationed far behind the lines. As regards the Jewish deportations, the reply was, 'Really, it is the first time I have heard about it.'

Three weeks later, however, the arguments shifted as the World Jewish Congress produced, with a great flourish, new documents. These were signed by Waldheim and proved beyond all reasonable doubt that his daily task was the collation of intelligence reports from all outposts of Army Group E. The data he collated contained information about the partisan war and the arrest of Jews. Other records showed that Waldheim had served at least twice in campaigns against partisans. These campaigns were noted for their atrocities. The presence of Waldheim's signature on intelligence reports exploded his denial of having any knowledge of atrocities, even if his personal participation in man-hunts was still to be proved conclusively. Moreover, from Greece came news that over a third of the population of Salonika was Jewish.

By the middle of April these documents could not be discussed by the Austrians with any degree of detachment. Their blood was up, and though Waldheim now began to look distinctly shifty in his answers, the Austrians, swept up on a tide of crude nationalism tinged with more than just a drop of anti-Semitism, closed ranks. They accepted Waldheim's nervous and clearly far from watertight answers.

To answer his critics' questioning of his ignorance about the Jewish deportations, Waldheim explained that army headquarters had been 'outside' Salonika and he rarely went to the town. He realized the excuse was fragile, and within a few days had changed his ground: 'Research has shown,' he told journalists, 'I was in Yugoslavia at this time.'

The web then became more tangled, for by this sudden admission he had, of course, only served to place himself in the midst of another big partisan-purging operation. This also dispelled any faith in the honesty of his original statement about 'being confined to a desk job'. Perhaps to escape, or perhaps because he really was confused, Waldheim told an exasperated correspondent for *The Times* that he was actually in Tirana (Albania) at the time.

Asked about his membership of the SA, Waldheim again resorted to his equestrian defence. This proved too much for the Austrian socialists, who for the first time began to press their attack home. Dr Sinowatz, a man not usually known for his wit, cracked the best joke of the campaign – and his career – when he said with a chuckle to horrified Austrian journalists, 'I accept what Herr Waldheim says; that he was not himself a member of the SA, only his horse was.' This remark, unusual in its acidity, unleashed a new wave of indignation among Waldheim's supporters, who had no time for such fencing.

Waldheim himself, though still unable to produce any documentary proof for his explanations, continued to bluster. 'I never saw a single partisan during those years,' he insisted tetchily. Continuing to ignore the intelligence reports he had signed, he addressed one Austrian audience after another, asking them to help him 'and our country'.

The World Jewish Congress, however, showed little sign of giving up the chase. Its general counsel, Eli Rosenbaum, flew to the national archives in Washington to 'hunt for the smoking gun'. A single document was all that was necessary to deliver the *coup de grâce*.

Beneath the rather unflappable exterior of Waldheim's advisers there was a definite whiff of panic. With the expert guidance of Heribert Steinbauer, a cool academic politician who was masterminding Waldheim's campaign, a distinct refinement of tactics began to take place. From now on, however well documented the allegations were, there was no question of any direct refutation or rejection. Instead the party paper gave great amounts of space to reports that Waldheim's successor at the United Nations, Javier Perez de Cuellar, had dismissed the accusations as 'ridiculous'. When contacted by the World Jewish Congress, Perez de Cuellar's office indignantly denied making the comment. But in Austria this denial was not given comparable coverage. Similarly, when a 1942 copy of the German army newspaper the *Donauzeitung*, which contained reports and a photograph illustrating the mass registration of Jews in Salonika, was found, Waldheim refuted the Congress's allegation that he would have read the report on the grounds that the newspaper was 'published in Bratislava, Czechoslovakia'. In fact, the paper was circulated throughout Yugoslavia and Greece, though there can be no guarantee that Waldheim read it. In Austria, however, this denial finally snapped the patience of those who had supported Waldheim's ignorance despite belonging to a different camp. Both Wiesenthal and Kreisky told reporters that they could no longer countenance that Waldheim knew nothing of what was happening in Salonika.

In Athens documents were released which shed more light on the transportation of the Jews from Salonika.

The papers, which had originally belonged to the German army, were published on 10 April; they showed that the intelligence unit in which Dr Waldheim served as section chief in July 1944 had issued the instructions for the deportation of Jews from the Aegean Islands. There were then about 1,700 Jews on the island of Rhodes. Only forty were to survive. Mr Joseph Lovinger, President of the Central Jewish Board of Greece, told a news conference he had obtained the papers from the World Jewish Congress.

One of these was a secret draft by the intelligence commander of the eastern Aegean, dated 15 July 1944, reporting details of a British naval commando raid on the island of Ikaria in mid-April by five uniformed Britons, led by a subaltern. These were helped in their mission by four local Greek civilians, who were named, most probably for further punitive action. The same document went on to hammer a further nail into the would-be President's coffin. According to paragraph 8, Jews were to be deported as follows: 'End of July deportation of Jews of non-Turkish nationality from all areas under the command, on instructions from High Command of Army Group E, Ic/AO. Execution by SD – Greece who have appointed a special unit for this purpose.' As Turkey was a neutral state at the time, its Jews were to be exempted from the order, but the instructions make it clear that Greek Jews would not be allowed such mercy. The document was addressed to the 'High Command of Army Group E, Greece Ic/AO'. According to an official table of organization, this was the intelligence unit in which First Lieutenant Waldheim was head of section 03 (one of four sections). This unit was entrusted, among other things, with intelligence briefings to the Chief of Staff of Group E, interrogation of prisoners and special tasks.

Army Group E was also the subject of other documents accompanying this one. One of these was a report dated 16 July 1944, bearing Lieutenant Waldheim's signature, which concerned British air raids on occupied Greece and action against Greek resistance. These documents powerfully supported Mr Lovinger's claims that at a time when 96 per cent of Salonika's Jewish population was going to be exterminated, Waldheim was stationed in the area.

Ominous rumblings on the Waldheim war record were to be heard in Belgrade as well as in Greece. Although Marshal Tito had personally decorated Waldheim in the years after the war, the papers in Yugoslavia always seemed to be the most incriminating. It is unlikely that Tito would have been unaware that Waldheim had served in the same theatre of war as his partisans. Perhaps the old Marshal, who had been party to so many atrocities himself during and after the Second World War, felt these things were best forgotten.

In any event, some years after the Marshal's death, the Belgrade archives produced an interesting file revealing that another Austrian officer, one Johann Mayer, had denounced Waldheim after the war for ordering reprisals against at least two Yugoslav villages, resulting in more than 100 deaths. This important piece of testimony was one of the reasons why Yugoslavia listed Waldheim as one of their wanted war criminals after the war. Unfortunately for those eager to catch Waldheim, the key witness, Mayer, could not be confronted with the evidence. He had died a few years earlier. His commanding officer, however, Lieutenant-Colonel Warnstorff, legally testified that Mayer was a liar. Later Warnstorff was to be a key contributor to Waldheim's 'White Book'.

With so many new allegations it was clear to all politically minded Austrians that the situation was rapidly deteriorating and that desperate measures had to be taken to refute the charges convincingly, otherwise all credibility would be lost. In crises Austrians are usually loathe to make up their own minds. Mental lassitude, together with the absence of any democratic traditions, makes the Austrians ill-equipped to deal with such situations. What is needed is guidance, and guidance from above.

This was now offered – somewhat reluctantly – by the Austrian President Dr Rudolf Kirchschläger. As a former lawyer and a man who enjoyed the respect of all parties, Dr Kirchschläger seemed the perfect man to deal with the question of Waldheim's war guilt. Though a socialist, he stood in the centre of the party and certainly had no particularly warm feelings towards any of the people involved. None the less, it should be remembered that the Austrian President had also served in the war with the German Wehrmacht and had obtained a higher rank than Dr Waldheim. At the end of the war Dr Kirchschläger had had to order young boys from the military academy at Wiener Neustadt to the front. Few returned alive. His obvious disagreement with Waldheim, who was then his superior, over the question of Czech visas in 1968 suggested that he would not be at ease with whitewashing the candidate.

With considerable excitement the Austrians tuned in to hear what the judge would now pronounce. That spring evening, for all its warmth, emptied the streets of Vienna. For once the *Heurigen* and the other traditional outdoor places of refreshment were deserted. The mood was similar, an elderly lady recalled, to the days when a rapt audience would await some announcement from the Kaiser.

The pronouncement, when it came, was something of a disappointment to all sides. In a languid voice laced with soporific vowels, the President went laboriously through the documents he had requested from the United Nations and those which the World Jewish Congress had collected for him. Rarely pausing to emphasize anything he said, it emerged only nebulously that in the President's opinion there was no 'conclusive ground', or *Beweis*, for believing his possible successor to have been engaged in anything worthy of the name 'atrocity'. At the same time, Dr Kirchschläger continued without pausing for a moment, it can be generally taken that he must have been aware of such activities. Predictably, both pro- and anti-Waldheim camps claimed a victory.

As he had gone through the 500-page dossier with almost painful thoroughness and dryness, most Austrians decided to take the President's words to mean whatever they wanted them to mean. The fact that the President had found no evidence that Waldheim had 'ordered' the reprisals overlooked, in the eyes of the

World Jewish Congress, their accusation that in his intelligence reports he had 'recommended' severe reprisals against civilians. Along the Ringstrasse the posters claiming Waldheim as the man the world trusts were now replaced by the jingoist phrase 'We Austrians vote for whom we want'.

Once again the Waldheim camp resorted to turning the issue towards what it called the 'grotesque motives' of those who had ordered the campaign against their candidate. At interviews he disarmed his opponents and journalists by a combination of bluff and outrage. One somewhat out-of-touch correspondent referred to this as 'the inimitable Viennese charm', but it was nothing of the sort. For journalists from other countries, interviewing Waldheim presented problems; not least among them was his inability to answer any question directly. This talent was highlighted during an interview he gave for BBC television. Attempts to force the man to answer the point were constantly deflected; insistence only resulted in a petulant display of temper and the demand that the interviewer 'be more objective'.

In this way document after document was brushed under the carpet. For the exhausted and incredulous World Jewish Congress, the ease with which Waldheim's myopia was tolerated was infuriating. 'Why,' asked an irritated Eli Rosenbaum, 'has no government demanded or even initiated an independent and properly funded investigation into Waldheim, rather than relying on our tiny team?' The reason seemed to be that, with the exception of a handful of surviving victims and their relatives, few people cared about what happened more than forty years ago.

So far the candidate had passed all trials with flying colours. The President, if not backing him, had not indicted him. Despite the roar of the World Jewish Congress, the governments of the West had not made any positively damning remarks. In fact, the entire controversy had brought out support for Dr Waldheim in some quarters. The Warsaw Pact countries and many Arab states defended Waldheim, criticizing their arch enemy Israel and condemning the United States for allowing the World Jewish Congress to attack 'so savagely the unsullied reputation of a world statesman'.

To the horror of the Socialist Party, the allegations had not stuck. Waldheim, who had always been the favourite, now seemed certain to win when the election was held at the beginning of May. A poll taken towards the end of April put his support at over 42 per cent. Another poll organized by an Austrian paper revealed even more alarmingly that, according to its researches, over 80 per cent of Austrians believed the allegations were linked with Waldheim's candidacy for the presidency and that 'therefore they could be discounted'.

Austrian military historians were brought out to testify that someone in as junior a position as Waldheim had been could never have undertaken reprisals. Ironically, this argument seemed the most suspect, as junior and non-commissioned officers in the German Wehrmacht enjoyed a responsibility far greater than that which existed during the war in the British, French or American armies. However, Waldheim himself resorted to this argument, though he never adopted the most obvious line of defence of all, which was simply that as he never rose above the rank of lieutenant throughout the war, he could not have been so very *engagé* to the Nazi cause. Perhaps this reasoning was too simple. Perhaps it would have offended those many Austrians who had fought in the war and were proud of it.

Far from dismaying the Austrians, Waldheim had allowed many of them, especially those of older years, to identify with him. '*I hab ah gekampft aah I bin kaa Nazi*,' an emotional postman remarked, explaining that though he had fought during the war, he was no Nazi. A long-suppressed emotion worthy of the analysis of Freud had been released, liberating skeletons which had gathered dust in many cupboards. What had been a private topic of conversation among friends and relatives now became a public theme, and Waldheim, through no action of his own, was riding the crest of its wave.

Throughout the country, especially in Graz, in Styria, and in Carinthia, another traditional right-wing heartland, the band for Waldheim played louder. In Vienna, where scepticism reigned all round, there was also hysteria. But the band which struck up one late April afternoon in the Graben at the centre of the city was not from an Austrian military unit blaring out the *Hoch und Deutschmeister*; it was that of the Royal Greenjackets. For a few days the all-consuming interest in the presidential campaign waned. The band struck up 'God Save the Prince of Wales'. Prince Charles and Princess Diana had arrived in Vienna for a three-day visit.

CHAPTER SIX

'NOW MORE THAN EVER'

The arrival of the royal couple, though a pleasant distraction for those who were rapidly wearying of the 'Waldheim affair', posed several problems of protocol for the British Embassy. Every manner of Austrian was lobbying the Ambassador and, according to one close confidant of His Excellency, some people were ringing him – just begging to be allowed to bribe him for a chance to meet 'Lady Di'. It was clear that for one Austrian there could be no question of meeting the Prince and Princess of Wales. As a prominent Austrian, there was no doubt that on any state occasion Dr Waldheim would have been presented to the royal couple, but this was out of the question. Harassed-looking diplomats were eager to point out that no meeting was scheduled. But if the doctor could not be photographed actually meeting the prince, some characteristic ruses could be employed so that they could at least see each other, even if no words were exchanged.

A concert had been organized in Vienna's Konzerthaus on the Ring for the second night of the royal visit. The programme was of traditional English fare; the Philharmonia was to perform Elgar's melancholy Introduction and Allegro for strings. The Viennese are normally contemptuous of British orchestras, believing that their beloved Wiener Philharmoniker is the best in the world and therefore the only orchestra worth listening to. They are even more dismissive of British music. Elgar is very small beer for an Austrian audience reared on Beethoven, Brahms and Bruckner, washed down with plenty of Mozart, Haydn and Schubert. Furthermore, no self-respecting Viennese would usually grace the comparatively modest Konzerthaus, preferring the more palatial and grand Musikverein, tickets for which are handed down generation after generation and where, despite a fall in standards here as elsewhere in Austria, conservative traditions remain triumphant.

Notwithstanding such reservations, the concert hall was packed. Who should be in the box opposite the royal couple but Dr Waldheim and his wife and daughter. It was a typical move. If the prince recognized the celebrity in front of him, he gave no hint. While the music played, Dr Waldheim seemed engrossed, eyes closed, in Elgar's harmonies. Mrs Waldheim stared at the box opposite, serious and unsmiling; perhaps there was something in such a quintessentially English sound which seemed inaccessible to a sensibility raised on a different kind of *klassische Musik*. Mrs Waldheim had joined the Nazi Party at the age of eighteen, and was often quoted in the Austrian press as being more ambitious than her husband. As she sat gazing at the couple opposite – so near and yet so far – it seemed to me there was a flicker of realization that many things would shortly be out of the Waldheim family's reach. At the interval members of the British community tripped over themselves in the mad dash to get into the reception for the royal couple; the doors were closed for the Waldheims.

'NOW MORE THAN EVER'

As the Prince and Princess of Wales toured Vienna, the international press was suddenly reminded of another side to Austria. The Vienna Boys' Choir, the Spanish Riding School and other traditional sights in the city momentarily eclipsed the Waldheim affair. But as soon as the royal couple departed, the press, both Austrian and international, resumed the story.

On 25 April a statement was issued by the U S Department of Justice, saying that it was going to study 'seriously' and 'comprehensively' recommendations that Waldheim be barred from the United States because of alleged involvement in wartime atrocities against Yugoslav partisans. The American Attorney General, Mr Edwin Meese, announced that he would be expecting to consider the recommendations over the following days. Austrian diplomats in New York looked on in disbelief as it was calmly announced that, under a section of the immigration law, foreigners who took part in Nazi war crimes could be prohibited from visiting the United States.

The recommendations were made by Mr Neal Sher, head of the Justice Department's Office of Special Investigations, which a few weeks earlier had been granted access to Waldheim's U N file. According to Sher, one of the files showed that Dr Waldheim had been 'special missions staff officer in the intelligence and counter intelligence branch' of Army Group E. According to leaked versions of Sher's report, Dr Waldheim had obtained 03 status, which meant that he was 'the third highest ranking special missions officer on General Löhr's staff'. No mean feat for a young lieutenant.

At this stage the Department of Justice was at great pains to point out that no decision to bar Waldheim had yet been taken. But the news from across the Atlantic was bleak enough. More details of Waldheim's Balkan career were emerging. In particular, the world now heard for the first time that the celebrated photograph of Waldheim standing to attention with an Italian general was in fact proof that he had been present at the planning of Operation Black at Podgorica (now Titograd) in Yugoslavia. This particular operation had been aimed at driving the partisans into submission through the seizing and execution *en masse* of civilian hostages. In May 1943 the operation killed more than 15,000 Yugoslavs.

Neal Sher made it clear that Waldheim and Operation Black were linked. 'Waldheim's claim that he was not involved in Operation Black is squarely contradicted by the photograph of him at the airfield at Podgorica. The operation began on May 15 and the meeting with the Italians at the airfield was a planning session,' Sher said. This news, which came barely a week before the election, predictably made little impact on the Austrians. Living in Austria, as those from other countries who work there are all too aware, is often like existing in a vacuum. The news bulletins are generally so concerned with local events that months can go by without one knowing what is occurring in the world at large.

The reasoning behind Sher's recommendation was certainly not given an airing in the Austrian media. Rather than mention Operation Black, Austrian papers preferred to dwell on what they insisted was a campaign of calumny.

The recommendation provoked a storm of protest from politicians supporting Waldheim. Herr Michael Graff, the tubby and abrasive deputy leader of the conservative People's Party, accused not the Department of Justice but the World Jewish Congress of continuing its 'hate-filled dishonest attack', thus implying a link between American Jewry and the recommendation. Graff went on to add that the report from the U S Justice Department was 'the indiscretion of someone in that ministry who is clearly friendly with a senior member of the World Jewish Congress'. Other conservative politicians took up this note. It was not a rational decision but 'horrifying behaviour' on the part of the Congress to persist in these 'infamous acts' after the balanced and calm judgement of President Kirchschläger.

Though the Austrian Foreign Minister, the socialist Leopold Gratz, ordered the Austrian Ambassador in the United States to investigate the report immediately, it was clear that no one else in Austria took the threat seriously. After all, if Waldheim had been allowed to live in the U S A for ten years during his tenure as Secretary-General of the United Nations, he would have to be allowed back now if the Americans were not to become a laughing stock. Few Austrians realized that the only country people would be laughing at in such a situation would be Austria.

The day after the reports from New York surfaced in Vienna, Waldheim, smiling and laughing, meandered through crowds of onlookers in the predominantly conservative Josefstadt, a pretty Biedermeier district of the city lined with early nineteenth-century *palazzi*. The presence of the Deutschmeister band, dressed in old imperial uniforms, added to the atmosphere of this most gentle part of Vienna, whose inhabitants still have something of the once famed Austrian charm. As the crowd gathered on the small square, listening to the strains of Strauss's Radetzky-Marsch, the tall gaunt figure of Waldheim suddenly emerged, clad in a faded Burberry mackintosh. The band stopped, the crowd was silent and Waldheim opened his arms in the now familiar claw-like gesture. This was the one gesture Waldheim had learnt for the campaign: whenever he was at a loss for something to say or something to do, he would just open his arms in a vast empty welcome. Like a puppet whose strings had been pulled once too often and were now stuck, Waldheim proceeded to spout his lines and adopt his poses automatically.

Associates of Waldheim's at the United Nations were fond of recalling how their boss had always learnt a set of lines, which he would use for any situation. Once, when he was on a United Nations famine inspection tour in Africa, he greeted a mother with a dying baby in her arms by telling her what a lovely child she had.

On this April afternoon it would be no different. The speech, like those at all of his meetings, had three elements: his defence (brief), his attack on the foreigners (long) and his bland generalities about policy (not so long). Because of President Kirchschläger's implied defence of Waldheim, the first part of the speech was now reinforced. In his dry and sombre pronouncement the President had dismissed all allegations that Dr Waldheim had been a war criminal. 'The affair against me has, my dear ladies and gentlemen, collapsed.' The assembled heads nodded, and Waldheim neatly skirted the one point which the President had raised against him: that 'he must have been well informed about the situation'.

Now it was time to attack the foreign lies. It was not the least ironic part of this entire affair that the man who had been billed as the Austrian the world trusted was so content to allow xenophobic rhetoric to enter into his speeches. 'You Austrians must vote for whom you want, not whom foreigners demand,' Waldheim again said and reiterated the old Nazi slogan, which had appeared on his election posters, 'Now more than ever'.

To tumultuous applause, Dr Waldheim said, as he had done many times before, that the attacks against him were an attempt to condemn an entire generation. 'I only did my duty. I only did what tens of thousands of Austrians were doing during the war.' A monocled man of sixty with a bronzed face looked on impassively, dressed in a tailor-made grey suit. As Waldheim moved among the crowd shaking hands, more and more young people stopped in the street to watch. I found myself next to the familiar inbred features of a young Archduke whom I had seen at parties in the country. We smiled, shook hands and watched the theatre before us.

What was so noticeable was that even though the speech was dull and not at all rabble-rousing or eloquent, it could still appeal to every conservative Austrian. Here was a man who was not a socialist. Here was a man in a smart suit with an international reputation, a Western European.

Speaking German, he cut a far more plausible figure than he did when shouting in thickly accented English to foreign journalists. The Archduke's family had certainly not fared well under the Nazis, but it was clear that in the vacuum of information which exists in Austria, the puppet in front was a credible and upright-looking fellow for any young conservative.

Wherever Waldheim moved, the same words met with the same reaction, nodding of heads and a vague feeling that despite all the hullabaloo, here was a man for the moment. Only once, a few days after the encounter in the Josefstadt, was the reaction different; it was in a very different part of Vienna.

On 29 April Waldheim appeared in Floridsdorf, the traditional working-class area of the city, where the Nazis strung up many of the Austrian conspirators in the plot to overthrow Hitler on 20 July 1944. Now as then it was a scorching hot day. Around Floridsdorf railway station it was clear that this was not a part of the city on the tourist route. No monuments, no cafés, just housewives, gypsies and eye-catching girls dressed in lurid colours. All were waiting to hear Waldheim make his first and only campaign speech in the heart of socialist Vienna.

'He's a Nazi, I know the truth!' shouts an old man in a tweed jacket, who was a little unsteady on his feet.

'Get rid of him. He's drunk,' some of the crowd cry, closing ranks. 'Go on, push off!' echoes the chorus of rather primly dressed ladies assembled near the microphone. The solitary protester is hustled away by a policeman as canned music drowns the murmuring crowd.

Dr Waldheim is late. Perhaps he suspects that Floridsdorf will give him a rougher ride than wealthier parts of the city. The crowd continues to grow. A Turkish *Gastarbeiter* spits out the end of a cheroot and nods approvingly. 'He's the only man with personality, a man of confidence,' he says, reflecting the Balkans' love of bravado, a quality Waldheim seemed to manifest to some people. A priest in a pin-striped suit and trilby nods assent and support for the Turk. 'He's the only man with international experience.'

The pro-Waldheim lobby in Floridsdorf is actually smaller than in other parts of Vienna, for the district is one of the poorest in the city and has a staunch socialist tradition. Nevertheless, as Dr Waldheim steps smiling out of his car, the crowd applauds. Before he can take more than two steps, the old man who shouted reappears as if from nowhere and promptly slaps the former United Nations Secretary-General on the face, sending him reeling back into his car. Someone shouts, 'Proletarian thug!' and for the second time the protester is bundled away by policemen. Unabashed but blushing a bright crimson, Dr Waldheim takes the microphone. 'For forty years I have been proud of this Austria,' he begins. 'We must return to co-operation and integrity and not the rules of the party book' – significantly, Waldheim plays down the socialist Jewish conspiracy and foreign demands. Floridsdorf demanded policies not accusations. 'That's what you all want!' Waldheim insists after a few meaningless sentences and the crab-claw pose. Judging by the cheers and applause, it clearly is what the normally socialist voters of

Floridsdorf want. There are some exceptions. 'Damn these Nazis; they are everywhere!' the protester, now sitting on a nearby lawn, mutters under his breath as Dr Waldheim steps back into his car and glides back across the Danube to the safety of Catholic, prosperous and conservative Vienna.

Floridsdorf excepted, it was a smooth ride through Austria on the campaign trail, and in that glorious spring week leading up to the May election, Waldheim went from triumph to triumph. From abroad too the news suddenly seemed to be encouraging. The rumblings of the World Jewish Congress had died down for the moment and some foreign politicians were tentatively supportive of Waldheim. The Chancellor of West Germany, Helmut Kohl, who was visiting Salzburg, broke the silence which had seized European statesmen when confronted with the affair. Speaking on Austrian radio, Herr Kohl suddenly announced that he had known Waldheim for years and that he was a 'great patriot'. 'I cannot vote in an Austrian election, but if I could I would certainly vote for Dr Waldheim,' the West German Chancellor said.

At the same time an opinion poll conducted by an independent Austrian company found that 60 per cent of the Austrian electorate considered it was 'irrelevant' that Dr Waldheim might be barred from entering the United States. He was still a 'perfectly respectable man' and Austria's reputation 'would not be tarnished' by his becoming head of state. According to the poll, 85 per cent of the electorate was critical of the World Jewish Congress and accused it of 'interfering with Austria's internal affairs'.

Such a hint of anti-Semitism was the cue Waldheim's campaign managers had been waiting for. As their candidate addressed meetings it was no longer just a case of 'We Austrians vote for whom we want'; now they said, 'We Austrians will not be dictated to by *einen Herrn Singer oder Herrn Bronfman*.'

The once stable and respectful air of politics in Austria began to evaporate and was replaced by a children's slanging match. One by one Austria's politicians began to criticize and accuse each other. An appeal by President Kirchschläger for a presidential election which would demonstrate Austria's 'democracy' went largely unheeded as some of the most bitter political exchanges in Austria's democratic history took place. The Austrian Chancellor, Dr Sinowatz, stood personally accused of masterminding a 'smear campaign' against Waldheim. For his part, Sinowatz accused his opponents, including Waldheim, of calculated lying and deception. Waldheim began to suggest that in the event of his being elected an apology from Sinowatz would be in order. Given that Chancellor and President are supposed to co-operate on so many issues, it became clear that if Waldheim were elected, there would have to be some smoothing of ruffled feathers.

As the mud-slinging went on, Waldheim, oblivious to all, set off for Carinthia and Styria to appeal to the voters of Austria's southernmost provinces. In Carinthia, where proximity to the Slavs and attempts by Yugoslavia twice this century to take over the province have fuelled a particularly fanatical breed of nationalist Austrian, Waldheim could be assured of a warm welcome. It was here that

Herr Jörg Haider, the charismatic pan-German, had carved a career and had attempted to segregate children into different schools, according to whether they were German-speaking or Slovene. The province's small Slovene minority had long grown used to Teutonic excess.

In Klagenfurt, the provincial capital, the usual bands and crowds gathered, and Waldheim with his wife walked among the crowd, offering a soft, almost silken, hand to the people while an aide took polaroid photos, which were handed to a delighted populace. But a more momentous event had occurred, and the crowds were smaller that May morning. The Austrians, like the rest of the world, woke up to hear about a nuclear reactor in a place called Chernobyl in Russia.

Nothing demonstrated the paternal society of modern Austria better than the way this disaster was handled by the Austrian media. Just as politicians closed their eyes to their pasts, just as exhibitions about great Viennese art before the Nazis set the cut-off date at 1934 rather than at the Anschluss of 1938, so too did the Austrian authorities turn a blind eye to Chernobyl. A gentle oily voice from the Scientific Meteorological Institute told radio listeners that there was 'not the slightest chance of the disaster affecting Austria'. In the Interior Ministry's duty room, a press spokesman asked what on earth Chernobyl had to do with Austria.

In Klagenfurt, however, the affair was immediately taken more seriously than in Vienna, and a group of schoolgirls who were to have presented Waldheim with a bunch of flowers were kept at home by their parents. In an emergency broadcast the Governor of Carinthia, Leopold Wagner, appealed for calm, and announced that the level of radioactivity was more than seventeen times the normal level. Despite the absence of the children, Waldheim continued on his way through the fruit market. Gradually, as the importance of the disaster in Russia dawned on him and the Austrians generally, it was curious to note the sudden introduction of environmental issues into his speeches.

From Klagenfurt Waldheim journeyed on to Graz, the capital of Styria and Austria's second largest city. Beautifully situated on the banks of the River Mur, it is off the beaten track, splendidly indolent and faintly Balkan in atmosphere. Its elegance, though unknown to all but the most discerning traveller, captured Napoleon's imagination when he stayed there on the way to Vienna. Unfortunately, for all its beauty and despite the sleepy atmosphere of a Habsburg *Pensionopolis*, Graz has always been a bastion of German nationalism. In the days of the empire, if regiments made up of Bosnians were stationed in the town, it often provoked pan-German rallies. Again, proximity to the Slavs encouraged Teutonic posturing.

Though most of the inhabitants are themselves 'assimilated' Slavs and possess the long limbs and long straight noses of the Slovenes, the culture in Graz, as the southernmost German city in Europe, has always had a Germanic edge. In the nineteenth century the town hall and many of the houses erected along the river were decidedly Germanic in inspiration: Nuremberg-style houses,

Spitzweg-inspired spires. When Hitler arrived in Austria in 1938, he received an overwhelming ovation from Graz – so great that he dubbed it the *Stadt der Volkserhebung*, or city of the people's rising. The Styrians had shouted, '*Ein Reich, ein Volk, ein Führer*' until they were hoarse.

Handsome but severe in temperament, with a dreaminess which all too easily flashes into fanaticism, they would be sure to back Waldheim. Yet because they placed much value on appearance, the support for Waldheim was not unqualified. He was a *Schwächling* (a softie). He looked shifty, and he might have done his duty, but he had only made it to lieutenant – what kind of a Nazi was that? On the one hand the Styrians welcomed a conservative who *had* a brown past; on the other hand, like the lowland Scot, they were sceptical of humbug and affectation. Waldheim for them was clearly a weak figure, and if they supported him in the following days, it was because they felt he was the victim of a 'Jewish campaign'.

As Waldheim wandered through a sea of expansive girls in dirndls and young men in grey Styrian *Tracht* with green facings, the air was markedly Teutonic. 'Of course we're anti-Semitic,' a young girl with a statuesque figure insisted when she was asked by foreign journalists about Austrian anti-Semitism. In a corner of the Herrengasse, a group of *Burschenschaften*, the students whose duelling and drinking combine with a taste for bright uniforms and faintly absurd hats, could be seen waiting to greet Waldheim. Such student groups are a familiar sight in most parts of southern Germany and Austria. In Vienna they hold a demonstration every year in front of the cathedral with posters and photographs illustrating the 'infamous evils of communism since the Germans were driven from Central Europe'. The boys are nearly all from lower middle-class backgrounds and have faces which, if stronger than those normally encountered in the country (especially among the vast aristocracy), are hideously deformed by the duelling scars. In Graz the number of such groups is very high, and in the streets around the university almost every inn has the letters and exclamation mark which are the signs that it is a meeting place for such groups. This is fertile ground for German nationalism and, in particular, the belief that the greatest war crime was not the destruction of the Jews but the driving of the Germans from Poland, Czechoslovakia and Yugoslavia. When an exhibition is staged in the Lower Austrian Palace of Government in the Herrengasse in Vienna on 'German' Moravia (now a province in Czechoslovakia), as happened a few years ago, one may by surprised by the nostalgia in the reminiscences of the older visitors. Such a calculated, officially condoned snub to the Czechoslovaks, underlines the problem an older generation feels in confronting its past. But when in Graz or Vienna one notices that a younger generation is seeing history through the same blinkered spectacles, surprise must turn to distinct unease.

As the election on 4 May loomed up, more disturbing than anything was Waldheim's undoubted appeal to younger Austrians, who irrationally and emotionally sought to protest against the socialists. The socialists were not smart; they looked like East European Stalinists; they were not chic. Waldheim had lived in America – he had to be chic.

Nothing illustrated this melancholy state of affairs better than Waldheim's last gathering in front of the cathedral in Vienna before thousands of young Austrians. But here, as if aware of the severe limitations of his own rhetoric, a veritable firebrand of a speaker was hauled on to the podium to rally the Austrians. Dr Kurt Dieman, a film producer with a bullet head and the stocky but energetic figure of Mussolini, took to the stage and delivered a speech which must count as one of the most remarkable ever heard in Vienna since the end of the thousand-year Reich. He immediately brought the crowds to silence, and then they heard one rousing and emotional climax after another. It was as if a new dictator had arrived. 'This great people . . . the glory of Austria . . . children of Andreas Hofer . . . children of the Babenbergs . . . this people are not a race of Nazis! . . . are not a people who need to ask for pardon!'

As this extraordinary display went on, delivered with dramatic gestures and ringing diction, it was hard not to think of Fascist Italy. When Waldheim himself finally reached the podium, his feeble words proved a great anticlimax, but by then, thanks to Dieman's speech, the audience was rapt and spellbound. They had witnessed as stirring a call to arms as that issued by Richard Hannay in John Buchan's *Mr Standfast*. Though, with its posturing, it was no doubt an inferior article, its result was the same. Waldheim proceeded to seduce Austrian youth. It was up to them to ensure that their parents would not be branded as criminals. It was up to them to save Austria from the dictates of Mr Singer or Mr Bronfman.

Mild hysteria and complete isolation from the attitudes of others make a dangerous combination. It was clearly what Waldheim was banking on and, with the die cast, he was soon to be proved right. Through his lack of sensitivity and his shrewd awareness of the weaknesses of the Austrian electorate, Waldheim had turned the tables on those who had sought to discredit him. By constantly exploiting the xenophobia of the Austrians, their limited historical perspective and above all their inability to see the other person's point of view, he had achieved a remarkable thing: the defiance of world opinion. No one who lived in Vienna at that time will forget the atmosphere of expectation. May 4 would be no ordinary day.

CHAPTER SEVEN

THE PRESIDENT IS ELECTED

Anyone who has never witnessed an Austrian general or presidential election cannot claim to have experienced all the bizarre fruits of politics. In Austria, where the parties fulfil their role as a paternal organization, the rallying of the troops is carried out with much largess and considerable thought for the comforts of the party faithful. On 4 May the *palazzo* opposite the Vienna opera house – the headquarters of the People's Party, which was backing Waldheim – opened its doors to thousands of supporters. From ten in the morning until well beyond midnight the wine flowed, along with beer and mineral water; there was a seemingly endless supply of frankfurters and rolls. In every panelled room food was consumed; on every parqueted floor the debris of field kitchens was visible. The focal points for all those present were the television sets in every room, which recorded in a series of coloured pyramids the state of the voting from minute to minute. On all sides, like aides-de-camp at a battle, young men rushed from one room to another noting details of the results as they came in: 2 per cent less in Kapfenberg, 0.5 per cent more in Eisenstadt. Each statistic wreaked its own havoc and confusion, before being corrected by another set of figures.

As the afternoon wore on, crowds began to gather outside the building. Waldheim and his managers were elsewhere. Only the urbane Heribert Steinbauer, the brain behind Waldheim's campaign, sat unperturbed in his office as telex after telex arrived congratulating him on what would certainly be his victory. In order to win, Waldheim would have to secure at least 50 per cent of the vote. If he didn't there would be a second election a month later: a run-off between him and his nearest rival.

In the event Waldheim polled 2,343,227 votes, an impressive total, but one which meant that only 49.6 per cent of the electorate had chosen to support him. His socialist rival, Dr Kurt Steyrer, polled just over 43 per cent. The result gave Waldheim a slightly larger lead than he had enjoyed in the opinion polls before the allegations emerged. Many Austrians had voted against him, though, and the socialist vote was strong enough to suggest that once the allegations had been made, the socialists had remained sceptical of Waldheim and true to their anti-fascist traditions. They suffered most at the hands of the Greens, who, led by the charismatic Freda Meissner Blau, a tall, grey woman, had capitalized on the after-effects of the Chernobyl disaster and had polled 5.5 per cent of the votes cast.

In the office of Waldheim's campaign manager, Steinbauer remained cool. 'At this very moment, we are printing the posters for the run-off, launching Waldheim as the Great Austrian.' Asked if he could cope with another month of Waldheim against the world, Steinbauer nodded assent. Afterwards he said he would recover in the Reading Room of the British Museum in London and begin taking Spanish lessons. A number of Western journalists wondered if this coolest and shrewdest of Austrians had taken leave of his senses under the strain of the last hours, but the next day, true to his words, the gigantic portraits of Waldheim were up.

Despite such confidence, rumours – always a danger in Austria – began to circulate that Waldheim's campaign had run out of steam. At any moment there might be further revelations, backed by more damaging evidence against him, which even the Austrians could not ignore. One of my articles, with the headline 'Why Waldheim has nothing to fear', provoked an anonymous letter from London warning that 'powerful evidence' was building up to prove that Waldheim had 'been involved with the interrogation and subsequent disappearance of British commandos in the Aegean'. However plausible this might have been, it seemed a particularly cranky way of commenting on an article which, in any case, had been critical enough of Waldheim. But the issue had long ceased to be domestic. One had to take into account that all manner of souls were now eager to grind axes of one sort or another.

In the socialist camp, any feeling that Waldheim might be running into difficulties was hard to detect. If the World Jewish Congress's allegations had not boosted the Waldheim vote, it was clear that they had not dented it either. The socialist candidate, the decent if dull Kurt Steyrer, had been outgunned by a sophisticated campaign, which had made a hero out of a most unattractive personality.

Steyrer's campaign boss, Peter Schieder, was quickly replaced by the Minister of the Interior, Karl Blecha, a bruiser of a man who, it was hoped, would inject some more bite into the campaign. In fact, the reverse took place, and Steyrer refused to attack Waldheim on his war record; he continued to talk about policies, something which by now few Austrians cared about. As one staunch socialist supporter sadly observed, 'If lemmings organized an election campaign, this is how they would do it.'

The deafening silence which the Socialist Party now cast over Waldheim's 'atrocities' was not, of course, matched by the World Jewish Congress. As they continued to attack the candidate, the ugly spectre of anti-Semitism, which had appeared just a few weeks earlier, became more evident. It was not that trains were suddenly daubed with swastikas and the words '*Juden raus*'. It was not the increase in threatening letters to Jews in Vienna. It was the fact that everyone began talking about anti-Semitism as if there were nothing particularly disagreeable about it.

Dr Steyrer said that every day he received letters accusing him of being involved in a Jewish conspiracy. The Austrian media also took up the theme, and suddenly this great unmentionable of Austrian life was being discussed alongside pensions and taxation. Waldheim and his supporters contributed to this development with remarks which competed with each other for thoughtlessness. Michael Graff, the General Secretary and deputy leader of the People's Party, accused the World Jewish Congress of provoking 'feelings that we all don't want to have'. It was left to the distinguished journalist Countess Barbara Coudenhove-Kalergi to point out that it was not a matter of whether you *wanted* to have those feelings, it was having them that counted. She said that the most painful thing in Austria was watching anti-Semites warn other anti-Semites against anti-Semitism.

Waldheim now addressed himself to this issue. 'I cannot be anti-Semitic,' he said. 'My English teacher was a Jew.' In the Palais Schwarzenberg, late in May, he talked of anti-Semitism, but it was too little and too late. Pandora's box had been opened. Nothing highlighted Waldheim's conspicuous lack of statesmanship more than his inability to confront the issue fairly and squarely and to say something about the life of those who had worked for a world in which decent, ordinary people would never have to confront the horrors of war. When he spoke of those who suffered in the war, he invariably referred to the Wehrmacht and the hundreds of thousands of Austrians who fought for the Reich. In the frescoed rooms of a palace whose owners had adopted Czech nationality rather than register as citizens of the German Reich in 1938, Waldheim warned against 'the new anti-Semitism'.

Other equally feeble gestures were to follow, always with the hint that this was a special favour for an under-privileged minority. The words '*Mitmenschen*' and '*Mitbürger*', which had never been used in the election, now filled his speeches. It was, of course, of little avail and provided small comfort to those who began to feel the backlash. In the Leopoldstadt, or the second district, where before the war over 100,000 Jews had lived, some orthodox Jews, on hearing a car screech noisily to a halt near them, panicked and ran. The car had only stopped because of a red light, but the atmosphere of those hot days allowed the pedestrians no chance for second thoughts. In the first district a small shop, which sold works of art by the Jewish people of the city and was prominently decorated with the Star of David, was now shut. A sign pinned to the locked door simply read: 'Closed because of threats.' Posters suddenly appeared near the botanical gardens in the third district; they called for a 'pure' Austria, and their cartoons portrayed orthodox Jews as capitalists supporting communism.

In the midst of all this unpleasantness, some of the more sensible members of Waldheim's entourage began to suggest that he should do more than just talk about anti-Semitism and should visit a synagogue. This proposal, however, encountered angry responses from many in the party who insisted, 'Why? He has nothing to apologize for.' This characterized the Austrians' attitude throughout May, and even if Waldheim's long career in diplomacy might have suggested to him that he should have made some grand gesture towards the victims of the Holocaust, the hard-liners in his party overruled it.

Many Jews in Vienna – there are only a few thousand left – uneasily continued to support Waldheim. Conservatives rather than socialists, they welcomed the support of Simon Wiesenthal, who continued to insist that there was no conclusive proof that Waldheim had committed atrocities. None the less, many were rattled by the country's mood.

Less than a week before the run-off, an interesting occurrence underlined vividly the support Vienna's most distinguished Jewish families continued to lend to Waldheim: the Dalai Lama arrived in Vienna. His Celestial Holiness was expected to give a long speech in the Haus der Industriellen Vereinigung, and a celebrity audience had gathered. Near the front sat a splendid lady, the descendant of one of the most famous Jewish families of the Austrian empire. While the last guests arrived, she lambasted the World Jewish Congress for their campaign against Waldheim. Just then a hush fell on the room and all heads turned, expecting to see the claret-robed God-King enter. Instead, in tripped Waldheim, ostentatiously late but beaming as he walked to the front row of seats. The lady, along with most of her companions, rose to give him a standing ovation. 'He is already our President as far as we are concerned,' she said with a smile. Only a distinguished novelist, who also serves at the Austrian Foreign Office, shuddered visibly at this comment and refused to rise.

It must be admitted that such Austrians were probably never going to be impressed by the case against Waldheim. In their book – and many of them had experienced the war – Waldheim, irrespective of his spinelessness, would be the first non-socialist President since the war. Outside such distinguished circles, however, the battle continued. At his major rallies a new figure appeared in the shape of the passionately emotional Frau Beate Klarsfeld, the celebrated German anti-Nazi demonstrator. Her attempts to disrupt his speeches at Linz and Vienna met with widespread disapproval. She was young, foreign and feminist, and therefore woefully ill-equipped to win the affection of the Austrians.

Meanwhile, in Belgrade, a new allegation was made in the magazine *Duga*. Waldheim's involvement with the Yugoslavs was a complex business; theoretically, they had the strongest reason to expose the man. Instead, he was decorated by Tito, and the files on him were suppressed. Although Simon Wiesenthal demanded in the first weeks of the presidential campaign that the Yugoslavs open their files on Waldheim, Belgrade had been conspicuously silent on the matter. *Duga* now published documents dating from 1943, when Waldheim was serving in the Balkans, showing what appeared to be Waldheim's signature on orders for harsh reprisals against civilians. The documents related to an order by Waldheim's commanding officer, General Löhr, demanding that at least fifty prisoners be shot for every German soldier killed. The documents bore what was said to be the countersignature of Dr Waldheim, and, if genuine, they would indicate that he must have been aware of atrocities in the Balkan campaign of General Löhr. This contradicted Waldheim's earlier statements that 'these matters were handled by other commands, certainly not by the staff I was attached to'.

Waldheim no longer answered allegations personally, and it was left to one of his staff to say that the documents were probably false and that 'it is impossible that Dr Waldheim could have had the power as a first lieutenant to order any reprisals'. This was still a flimsy argument. In the Wehrmacht, if the officers were out of action, a corporal would often lead a unit in an emergency; it was not inconceivable that a subaltern might be called upon to perform duties normally reserved for field officers.

As news of these documents surfaced in Austria, historians began to wrangle over whether Waldheim's signature on such a document would be a mere formality and would not 'necessarily concern personal involvement'. It was clear, coming at this late stage, that nothing was likely to shed any new light on Waldheim's career or influence his chances of becoming elected. The hatches were now battened down all over Europe for his inevitable election. The French were rumoured to be cracking their best brains over a telegram which could congratulate Waldheim without offending Jewish opinion in France. A senior British diplomat said that 'The Austrians are very stupid', but that there were no grounds for him to advise his country to treat them any differently. In America, the Department of Justice, which had raised the possibility of barring Waldheim from entering the USA said that it would await the result of the election before taking any decision. The Austrians, naturally, just dismissed this as a vague foreign threat; the party could not be stopped now.

Only in the Seittenstättengasse, where the Vienna Jewish Cultural Community had its headquarters, were there reservations. There a spokesman for the community insisted that whoever won the election, there would be no congratulatory telegram. Neither result could alter the fact that for the first time since the Nazi era anti-Semitism had been used as a means to political ends.

Such bitter reality was remote from the Palais Todesco,

where once again the party faithful were gathered for the victory which had been denied them the month before. Perhaps because victory seemed certain, many groups gathered which had been absent at the first election in May. Throughout the campaign, any impartial observer would have been struck by the extraordinary contrasts among Dr Waldheim's supporters. On that bright summer's day every corner in the city seemed to underline this.

Vienna at the weekend is a ghost city. The inhabitants flee the fog of winter or the dust of summer and invade the neighbouring woods and *Heurigen* in search of wine and some mild but not too strenuous exercise. This Sunday was no different, and Vienna took on its usual stage-set appearance: heavy overpowering Ringstrasse buildings dwarfed the few pedestrians to be seen on the cobbled streets. As I hurried to the Palais Todesco, an old, six-foot-six-tall Count, who had been educated in England long before the war and had fled the Nazis in 1938, drifted out of the Hotel Sacher. Had he voted, I asked. Of course, he replied, he was voting for Waldheim. He personally despised him; he had worked with him and loathed him and had found the Nazis in 1938 so objectionable that within weeks of the Anschluss he had had to abandon Vienna or be arrested. For him, the question of Waldheim's politics was more important for Austria than his integrity. Moreover, not to have voted for him would have been to condone the socialists and their allies, who, in the Count's opinion, had certainly been behind the appearance in the USA of the documents concerning

Waldheim's career. He marched off, a handsome, gaunt figure, in the direction of his club and disappeared under the arches of the Augustinerkirche.

How very different from this cool, rational and dignified figure were the younger members of the vast Austrian aristocracy who now clambered up the stairs of the People's Party headquarters. As Nancy Mitford wisely wrote, an aristocracy in a republic is like a chicken whose head has been cut off; it may run about in a lively way, but in fact it is dead. In Austria, where the aristocracy was always a more decorative than useful element of society, the decline is particularly marked in the younger generation. As early as 1945, Missie Vassiltchikov in Vienna noted in her diaries the 'enormous difference' between the generation of Austrian aristocrats who still ran an empire and the 'present generation, who grew up in an amputated, stunted little country with no future. The latter are, nearly all of them, basically provincial and even when there is still plenty of money around, they can barely speak a foreign language. They are by and large lightweights with few of the fundamentally solid qualities that still characterize good Germans.'

In 1986 such remarks could be made *a fortiori* and in the hall of the Palais Todesco a clutch of these latter-day 'lightweights' hailed me. Foolish grins and a smug conviction that they were experiencing their country's 'greatest day' mingled with a feeble violence which reminded me of demented sheep. They were a stark and worrying contrast to the fine old man I had seen emerge from the Sacher. There is perhaps nothing more worrying in Austria today than its youth. On every front, in every stratum of society, it manifests the conspicuous failure of an older generation to address itself to the future or confront the past. The young Austrians, after all, owe their crassness and shaky attitudes to the generation which has so woefully failed to bring them up properly.

Most of the young *Grafen* lounging around had learnt at school, along with many other teenagers in Vienna, that Hitler was a 'socialist revolutionary and a military genius', nothing more. At the smarter schools in the city they would have enjoyed anti-Semitic and racial jokes in class and would have filled their end-of-term revues with such things. Later, at university, they would study for years, leading a life of indolence which would horrify any northern European or American. Pampered at home and by the very socialist state they wished to destroy, the merest hint that their pensions might be in jeopardy come the year 2030 would be enough for them to grumble and go on strike. Heaven help Austria should this generation ever have to show some responsibility and tighten its belts. Unlike the young people of West Germany, who know all too well the horrors their countrymen perpetrated this century and who are the great hope of that country, the young Austrians never reached any rational confrontation with the past. Now their ideas about the past would be vindicated: the Nazis had only done their duty; there was such a thing as a world Jewish conspiracy; the press was dominated by Jews.

Gradually, as the results began to pour in, it was clear that Waldheim's majority would be increased, and

◁ Adolf Hitler returns to his homeland and acknowledges the saluting crowds in Vienna, 1938

▽ Hitler's birthplace in Braunau am Inn

▽ The Vienna men's hostel where Hitler lived between 1909 and 1911. The hostel was opened by the Emperor in 1906, when this photograph was taken

△ Dr Waldheim grew up in a chaotic and unstable Austria, ravaged by political unrest. This photograph shows wounded Nazis being handed out of the Vienna broadcasting station after violence following the assassination of Chancellor Dollfuss in 1934

▽ Even before Hitler became Chancellor, fears of a Nazi coup in Germany led to anxiety among the authorities in Austria. Here barbed wire is placed in the streets of the frontier town of Salzburg, May 1933

Vienna
Dated February 15, 1938
Rec'd 12:32 p.m.

Secretary of State.
Washington.

Rush.
20, February 15, 1 p.m.
My telegram February 14, 9 p.m.

Dined last night at a large dinner given by Schmidt with Chancellor Schuschnigg, Seyssinquart, members of the Government and diplomatic corps. Atmosphere most oppressive. To French Minister Schuschnigg described visit to Berchtesgaden as the most horrible day of his life. He says that Hitler undoubtedly a madman with a mission and in complete control of Germany. Hitler openly told him of his desire to annex Austria and declared that he could march into Austria with much greater ease and infinitely less danger than he incurred in remilitarization of the Rhineland. Schuschnigg admits that appointment of Seyssinquart is highly dangerous but states that he will make it in order to avert the "worst." In respect of Italy, Schuschnigg declared that he can count only on moral not material support.

Schuschnigg is attempting to make best of bad situation and was in a long and friendly conversation with Seyssinquart. Hornbostel is in utter despair and states openly that there is nothing left for him to do but to leave Foreign Office.

Italian Minister claims that he was informed of Berchtesgaden meeting only on the eleventh and denied that Italy took any initiative in the matter. He telegraphed full information to Mussolini. Latter however is engaged in winter sports and up to last night Chigi had no information that his messages had reached the Duce. Italian Minister gives anxious impres[illegible].

[illegible] Papal Nuncio adm[illegible] that Sey[illegible]inquar[illegible] be good Catholic
[illegible]rs [illegible]thele[illegible]

△ A telegram, dated 15 February 1938, from the US Consul-General in Vienna, John Wiley, which graphically describes the atmosphere in the country

▽ Demonstrations by rival groups were frequent on the streets of Vienna. Here Catholic scouts pass through the streets in May 1934

▽ Carinthians celebrate on the Heldenplatz in Vienna. A particularly fanatical breed of nationalist Austrian grew up in the province of Carinthia

△ Four-power control of the country lasted till 1955. The Soviet guard marches past the monument of Prince Eugen on the Heldenplatz, December 1953

▽ British military police hold back the celebratory crowds as the flags of the four nations are lowered at the Allied Commission Building, July 1955

△ Bruno Kreisky, socialist Chancellor of Austria through the 1970s. Dr Kreisky was imprisoned twice in the 1930s and escaped to Sweden in 1938

▽ Fred Sinowatz became Chancellor in 1983. He was a native of Austria's most easterly province, Burgenland, and to some Austrians his appointment personified the Balkanization of the country

△ Chancellor Franz Vranitzky, who said in February 1988 that he would continue in office only if 'the Waldheim affair' didn't continue to take up sixty per cent of his time

▽ Dr Waldheim triumphs at the 1986 presidential election. His beaten rival, the socialist candidate and former Health Minister, Kurt Steyrer, tries not to look too disappointed

Below: Waldheim (*right*) in uniform during the war. *Above*: Waldheim (*second from left*) at a meeting in May 1943 at an airstrip in Podgorica, Yugoslavia.

△ Graffiti on the ubiquitous election posters: 'Defamation shall not pay off! Therefore Waldheim' and 'Fairness for Waldheim'

▷ Waldheim, now President, visits the site of Mauthausen concentration camp in northern Austria, August 1987

△ Waldheim in 1955: taking his seat as Austria's delegate at the UN

▽ Thirty years later: on the presidential campaign trail in Vienna, April 1986

euphoria erupted among the frankfurter-eating television viewers, who on their screens saw one black column after another rising above the socialists' red ones. Upper Styria had voted for Waldheim! Cries of ecstatic enthusiasm now rattled through the building, for Upper Styria, with its mining industries, was a traditionally socialist stronghold. By nightfall a jazz band had gathered outside and was playing a famous Frank Sinatra song, while young Austrians sang 'We'll vote for Waldheim' as the refrain instead of 'I'll do it my way'. The party was now on in earnest, and once again the contrast between friendly euphoria and xenophobic suspicion, all in the same room, was marked. Could all these friendly jolly people in their *Tracht* and *Lederhosen* really harbour Nazi feelings? As is often the case in Central Europe on such occasions, it was the girls who took to the hysteria with more relish than the men. Austrian girls have a reputation for finding a romantic adventure difficult to resist. They tend to be more impressive than Austrian men, possessing, perhaps through years of being treated with contempt, a strength of character that often eludes their male counterparts.

As the evening wore on and it emerged that Waldheim's majority had risen to 7.7 per cent, strikingly dressed girls mingled with the crowds, hungry for adventure. Rich women appeared in expensive dirndls, and a sprinkling of chic girls wore the latest fashions. One statuesque blonde beauty suddenly appeared in a dark-blue mackintosh asking to see Alois Mock, the leader of the People's Party. While an eager, if inebriated, aide went off in search of the worthy but lacklustre Herr Mock, the girl confided that this was the greatest day of her life and that she was keen to – as she put it – 'rape handsome Herr Mock'. Under her mackintosh she wore only black suspenders and a long black sweater. Setting off this devastating outfit was a pair of black kid gloves which, she insisted, she would *never* take off. Once again the apotheosis of unreality was at its height.

As the young beauty rushed off to exchange words with Herr Mock, a celebrated Austrian journalist came up; he said he was 'determined to get smashed'. The editor was a likeable anglophile and certainly no anti-Semite – his wife was Jewish – but he was intoxicated by Waldheim's success. The socialists are finally on the way out in Austria, he eagerly asserted.

As a Lower Austrian band playing military marches mounted the stairs, the man of the moment appeared, strictly watched by scores of plain-clothes policemen. In a brief speech to his supporters, Dr Waldheim attempted to sound jubilant. The election result was Austria's answer, he said, to his appeal for a return to 'fairness, morality and Christian values'. Later he said his lawyers had been instructed to investigate accusations that he was linked to war crimes; he would use his personal contacts in America to deal with any problems there. No hint was given that anything but the mildest problems awaited Austria in her immediate future. Waldheim was now President, and things would inevitably calm down.

Such is the astonishing naïvety of those who live in a world of fantasy. Once again the baroque had triumphed. The Austrians had a President who mirrored their own complicated vision of reality, the President they deserved. That, however, was not to be the end of the matter.

CHAPTER EIGHT

DAMAGE LIMITATION

Within twenty-four hours of Dr Waldheim's being elected, political fall-out from the result began to make itself felt throughout the country. For the first time since the affair blew up it now appeared that the consequences for Austria's political life would be as serious as those for the country's relations abroad. Despite no fewer than three weighty leaders in *The Times* warning the Austrians that Waldheim's election would mean that Austria could no longer consider itself part of the Western world; despite the warnings of diplomatic and economic isolation and that, in the inimitable phrase of the *Daily Mail*, 'like Austria's wine, Waldheim will not be able to travel', the Austrians had wanted a change and had chosen their man. Change indeed was now swift in coming.

For a few weeks it had been clear that the relationship between the new President and Chancellor Sinowatz would be fraught with difficulties. Waldheim had said he wanted Sinowatz to apologize for implying he was a liar. Supporters of Waldheim's party were already uncovering evidence that Sinowatz and his associates were behind the campaign to 'defame', as they called it, Waldheim's name. Clearly the Ballhausplatz would be too small for both of them. The following day Sinowatz resigned.

As a few other socialist ministers also threatened to resign, to most Austrians' surprise their choice of

Waldheim was being justified far sooner than they could ever have dreamt was possible. The hateful and 'unsightly' Sinowatz was gone, his henchmen and other extreme left-wing politicians were also on the way out and the socialists were rattled, assuredly doomed in the general election four months away. Though Sinowatz attempted to tell his supporters that his decision to resign had not been due to Waldheim's victory, it was clear after a five-hour emergency meeting of the party bosses in the Parliament that the hunt for scapegoats was on and blood would have to be spilt.

Speculation was rife that the socialists could only win the next general election if they were prepared to make a drastic change to their image. This they proceeded to do. Sinowatz's replacement was the relatively inexperienced but capable Franz Vranitzky, a 49-year-old, pin-striped banker who had only become involved in Austrian politics two years earlier when he left his job to become the country's Finance Minister. At a stroke, then, the ideology of the most powerful political party had been changed. Not for the first time, the socialists proved that they were a more dynamic party than their rivals and that despite their size, they were susceptible to change and could adapt themselves to the *Zeitgeist*.

Sinowatz was dropped, unmourned and unloved, and yet, even though his alleged links with the passing of Waldheim's files to the United States suggest a ruthless and ambitious operator, he had done his best to steer his country through its most difficult few years since it became independent in 1955. When Kreisky had refused to remain Austria's Chancellor after the Socialist Party lost its overall majority in parliament three and a half years earlier, Sinowatz agreed only with reluctance to become head of the Socialist–Freedom Party coalition government. Eschewing his predecessor's high profile in international affairs, Dr Sinowatz chose wisely, though unpopularly, to adopt a less patrician pose, using his broad acceptance in the party to hold together an increasingly crisis-ridden government. A gifted improviser, whose humble origins in Burgenland gave him a distinctly Balkan approach to politics which was well suited to the almost ceaseless intrigues of Austrian political life, Sinowatz's footwork and presence in the coalition without doubt restrained deep divisions from coming to the surface in his party. The presence of the right-wing and incompetent Freedom Party in his government provoked problems that his illustrious predecessor never faced. Few Austrian politicians could have held his government together as well as he did during the storm which blew up when his Defence Minister shook hands with the repatriated war criminal, Walter Reder.

Needless to say, his appeal to the World Jewish Congress, which at that time was meeting in Vienna, was considered with some scepticism by many Austrians. Claiming that he himself was not anti-Semitic, Sinowatz had told the Congress a story about how all his family had cried so much during the *Kristallnacht* when neighbouring Jews were dragged away that the children had to be given lots and lots of chocolate to stop weeping.

The removal of Sinowatz did not have any effect on

the international outcry which followed Waldheim's election, but the Austrian press ignored the rumblings beyond its frontiers. The chief of these, predictably, were to be heard in Israel. The Israeli Ambassador in Vienna, Michael Elitzur, was recalled to Jerusalem for consultation. Elitzur had been due to end his term of service in Vienna that summer, but it now seemed unlikely that he would return to Vienna. Rumours began to circulate in the city that he would certainly boycott Waldheim's inauguration ceremony a month later. The decision to recall the envoy was taken at a meeting between the Israeli Prime Minister, Shimon Peres, and Yitzhak Shamir, the deputy Prime Minister and Foreign Minister. They agreed that the question of a replacement would be discussed, but they conceded that there was considerable opposition to sending anyone at all.

The Austrian Ambassador in Israel, Otto Fleinrat, was given the frosty message that the Israeli Foreign Ministry noted 'with deep regret and disappointment the election result and that it had been hoped that the choice of a man with a past like Waldheim's' could have been prevented. Fleinrat replied, drawing on the formidable expertise of Austrian diplomacy, that 'as the position of Austrian president is only ceremonial, there is no need for relations between the two countries to be affected'. While the Israeli Foreign Ministry acknowledged that there was not yet a complete case against Waldheim and that they had every intention of maintaining good relations with Austria, there was an increasing number of calls in the Knesset for a boycott of Austria. The right-wing Tehiya Party warned that it would launch a campaign to stop tourism to Austria.

In America the reaction was similarly mixed. Jewish leaders angrily denounced Waldheim's election and asked the US Attorney General to place him on the Justice Department's 'watch list', which would bar him entry to the USA. But President Reagan sent a normal message of congratulations to the newly elected President. Larry Speakes, his spokesman, said, 'The people of Austria have made their choice in a free and democratic election.' The USA would continue its close friendly relations with Austria. The American Jewish Congress was less impressed. By electing a man with a Nazi past, the majority of Austrians had 'knowingly and deliberately associated themselves with that past'. Notes of disapproval were also struck by Jewish organizations throughout Europe.

Only in Eastern Europe and the Soviet Union was Waldheim treated to some praise, albeit of the kind he could have well done without. In Moscow the Soviet authorities, widely criticized abroad for the treatment of their own Jewish population, sprang quickly to Waldheim's defence; they alleged he was the victim of an 'unseemly' campaign aimed ultimately at discrediting the United Nations. Tass, the official Soviet news agency, was fulsome in its praise for Dr Waldheim's performance during his ten years as UN Secretary-General. It claimed that Israel had already admitted that it had no evidence that he had been involved in any war crimes. The Soviet Union's praise for Waldheim raised several questions. Even if Waldheim welcomed it, it was certainly not good news for the Austrians who, bordered on three sides by communist regimes, have little but loathing for and fear of Moscow.

Meanwhile, in Vienna more heads began to roll in the wake of Waldheim's victory, which kept the Austrians distracted from foreign comment on the events of the previous days. Dr Leopold Gratz, the socialist Foreign Minister, swiftly followed Sinowatz into the background of the party by resigning his ministerial post. It could be argued that the job was now the most difficult in the entire cabinet. The position was seen as being of vital importance to good relations between the Chancellor and the President. Gratz, for all his *bonhomie*, was too closely associated with Sinowatz to remain.

Into the breach stepped another socialist on the right wing of the party, another man who wore pin-striped suits and knew something of the world: the gifted Dr Jankowitsch. He was to provide an admirable, if fleeting, glimpse of the deep layers of talent within the Austrian Socialist Party. Jankowitsch's first task was to mobilize his diplomats into defending the democratic decision of his country. This was more difficult than might have been expected, but it briefly deflected the wrath of the World Jewish Congress, which now turned towards the United Nations files.

'If you hide the past, you will bury the future,' Benjamin Netanyahu, Israel's Ambassador to the UN, had said when referring to a gloomy repository on Park Avenue South, New York, where he believed the United Nations was hiding its past. The repository contains in excess of

40,000 general files. There are more than 25,000 referring to individuals accused of war crimes by the seventeen-nation UN Commission set up to investigate the subject after the war. For nearly forty years successive UN administrations have sought to deny access to these files, except to individuals or countries with a genuine (whether legal or scholarly) interest in their contents. Only three files – those on Eichmann, Barbie and Mengele – have been released in any way that might be called full. The items in this massive archive are not believed to refer to casual or insubstantial accusations. They refer, rather, to instances where there was at least a prima-facie case to be pursued. 'You must face it,' Netanyahu insisted, 'this is where you will find the record.'

While the World Jewish Congress vowed to crack open these files, maintaining that they would never permit the Waldheim affair to fade from the public consciousness, the protagonist of the entire business prepared himself in Vienna for his first major confrontation with the press since his victory. The Concordia Press Club, a distinguished old building in the heart of Vienna, which, though supposedly a club for journalists, lacks a bar and is shut at 6 pm, was packed that morning. From America and Holland, Scandinavia and even India, television crews thronged through the doors. Waldheim, when he arrived, was brisk and businesslike. Beaming like a Cheshire cat, he gave his most cogent and clear condemnation of anti-Semitism in Austria to date. But again it seemed too little too late. Why had he not been more outspoken during his campaign? Did he feel that had he made some gesture then, he would have lost votes and that now, with the voting safely over, he could embark on a sudden tirade against anti-Semitism? It would be agreeable to think otherwise, but such cynicism comes easily to anyone who has observed Austrian politics at close quarters over a period of time.

Irrespective of motive, Waldheim was on fighting but magnanimous form. 'The terror of the Holocaust should not be forgotten,' Dr Waldheim said, adding that the media campaign against him was 'understandable in the light of the horrors of that time'. He would soon visit the site of Austria's principal concentration camp at Mauthausen on the Danube. Once again the seasoned observers of Austrian politics found themselves asking why he had not done this earlier.

Though his staff attempted to persuade the journalists present that they should address themselves to the problems of Dr Waldheim's future, he faced a barrage of questions about his past. In particular, the case of the British commandos who disappeared in the Aegean was raised time and again. Despite the claims of evidence by several British MPs, Waldheim fielded these questions with a mixture of outrage and charm, insisting that he had never even seen a British prisoner of war during his time in the Balkans. When asked what he felt like when he had initialled orders for reprisals against civilians, Waldheim merely pulled rank and said to the young Americans present, 'You are too young to remember the war. Gentlemen, war is war.' The fact that the war under discussion had been a completely different war from any other fought in recent history seemed to escape Waldheim, as it did many of the other correspondents present.

The past having been dealt with so effectively, similar detachment from reality was employed with regard to the future. Yes, the new President was eager to visit America and was consulting the authorities and lawyers over whether there would be any difficulties. 'I hope to visit all the signatory states of the Austrian State treaty,' he said with a smile. The President also insisted that many countries had congratulated him. Support from the Arab world had been overwhelming, he said, but he refused to be drawn on what his response would be to Colonel Gaddafi's congratulatory telegram which praised him for 'striking a blow against Zionism.' His optimism was summed up by his repeated phrases: 'I have nothing to fear and I welcome any efforts to clarify problems.' He backed, in particular, Simon Wiesenthal's call for an international historical commission to go through all the relevant documents concerning his wartime career. 'They will see that I, as a mere Leutnant, had no *Schiessbefehl*' (order to shoot).

The conference broke up, and all eyes now turned to the formal swearing-in of the President, which would occur in a few weeks and which diplomats would or would not attend. Hopes were high in the country that, in the tradition of all Austrian presidents since the war, Waldheim would remain above controversy. The day before the ceremony of 8 July such wishes were shattered by the disclosure that the ceremony would be boycotted by both the American Ambassador and the Israeli

Embassy. Socialist MPs also said they would not be there. The American Ambassador, Ronald Lauder, a prominent member of the wealthy Jewish family whose fortune is founded on cosmetics, could not attend for 'family reasons', but this was widely interpreted as a snub and as confirmation of rumours that Lauder wished to spend as little time as possible in the presence of Waldheim.

As the dignitaries of those embassies who were making less fuss about it made their way to the Parliament, a newly discovered wartime document released in Jerusalem showed that 2,500 Jewish men, women and children were deported to the Auschwitz extermination camp on the order of the German army unit in which Waldheim served as the deputy chief intelligence officer. This new document had been discovered in the Federal archives in Freiburg, West Germany. Dated 22 September 1944, it records: 'deportation of Jews end of July 1944. Deportation of Jews not holding Turkish citizenship in the entire command territory upon instructions of the High Command of Army Group E, Ic/AO.' This concerned the Jewish population on the islands of Crete and Rhodes. In a letter sent to the US Department of Justice the previous April, Dr Waldheim had said he was the 03 officer of this unit. This meant he was responsible for operational intelligence and control of the intelligence staff.

Members of the World Jewish Congress were not slow to exploit this and its director, Elan Steinberg, said that the new evidence should be considered by the American authorities, who should place the Austrian President elect on the watch list. Steinberg went on to say that the document refuted Waldheim's claim, in a letter he sent to the President of the Congress, Edgar Bronfman, on 7 March, that he had 'never been informed' about the deportation of Greek Jews. To mark Waldheim's inauguration as President, the Knesset gave a special showing of *Shoah*, a nine-hour film about the Holocaust.

The ceremony in the Vienna Parliament was a far from pleasant experience. The Parliament is perhaps the finest building on the Ringstrasse. Designed by the architect Theophil von Hansen in a rich, neo-Grec style, it has a hall of magnificent Corinthian columns made of fabulous marble. Unfortunately, some of the rooms were bombed and the frescos they once possessed were not always restored, so that certain rooms have an almost twentieth-century neo-classical atmosphere. Into one of these sombre interiors marched Waldheim, noticeably less buoyant than he had been a few weeks earlier. Perhaps the fact that he was reaching what was for him the apogee of his political career now overwhelmed him. Perhaps in the few weeks between his optimistic press conference and the ceremony he had realized that his battle was by no means over. In any event, he proceeded to deliver an extraordinary speech, which for hypocrisy, historical inaccuracy and self-inflated bombast had few rivals.

Sitting in front of him in a single line, their hands clasped together like prisoners in a dock, were the members of the government, weary and resigned to despair. Beyond them, in the front row of the MPs, sat a glowering Fred Sinowatz. He wore a look of high dudgeon throughout the proceedings, his face even darker than its usual swarthy shade of brown.

Only once was there a hint of humour: the new Chancellor, Vranitzky, raised his eyebrows with detached scepticism when Waldheim referred to him and his men as needing to be a 'government which can govern'. Not far from Vranitzky sat Waldheim's defeated socialist rival, Kurt Steyrer, also tanned after a long holiday beneath an equatorial sky. Steyrer had to listen to Waldheim's effusive thanks for his 'personal fairness' during the campaign. This woke up some nodding MPs, and they caught a glimpse of Steyrer, who returned their glances with a stare which could most charitably be interpreted as one of curiosity.

Dr Waldheim also referred to the 'Austrian patriots' who 'disappeared, never to be seen again' when the Nazis marched into Austria in 1938. This inevitably produced more raised eyebrows among the socialist politicians, many of whom shook their heads with disbelief when Waldheim went on to refer to the tragedy which befell Austrian Jews under the Third Reich. Diplomats whispered and Dr Waldheim's supporters exchanged knowing nods during the silence that followed his statement that 'the liquidation of these people cannot be forgotten'. Only a team of American television journalists, incongruously dressed in blue suits which clearly did not belong to them, remained impassive, chewing gum.

Predictably, Dr Waldheim's speech ended on a note of patriotism, the factor which had contributed so much to his success. Austria, he said, found itself in a tricky but none the less favourable situation, rich in opportunity. 'This fine people of seven million, who have never caused any disturbance in the world, can walk into the future in a spirit of general solidarity and brotherhood,' the President said, rounding off his speech to tumultuous cheers from the conservative MPs who had backed him throughout.

Outside the Hofburg the scene was no less tumultuous, though for different reasons. Demonstrators, many of whom seemed middle-aged rather than young, gathered on the Ring. In front of the Chancellery on the Ballhausplatz men dressed in the striped clothes of concentration camp inmates carried large placards, on which were pasted photographs of Waldheim in Wehrmacht uniform. Banners which proclaimed, 'We do not want a war criminal for President' were unfurled briefly, before being put away on the instructions of the police. The most picturesque member of the demonstration was a twelve-foot-tall wooden horse, an ironic reference to Waldheim's membership of a Nazi riding club before the war. From deep inside its papier-mâché belly a loudspeaker called out, 'I am a horse trusted by the world.'

For those who wished to demonstrate against the decision of the majority of the electorate, such events seemed at first the only option. In fact, many Austrians who found the election of Waldheim distasteful had already begun to organize themselves into a protest group. Artists, writers and intellectuals formed what was almost a new party, only it had no pretensions to power. '*Neues Österreich*', or New Austria, was founded to help clean up Austria's image in the aftermath of the election and show the world that there were some Austrians who did not support Waldheim. Stickers appeared on cars claiming simply, 'I didn't vote for him.' Outside the Chancellery and the cathedral small demonstrations consisting of old Austrian socialists on a hunger strike 'until Waldheim resigns' also began.

Waldheim's office dissociated itself from such events, which were regarded in the media as the activities of a lunatic fringe. It pursued instead its own initiatives. It was clear even to the most fervent supporter of the new President that it would be very difficult for him to travel in the West. In a bid to mend its damaged fences with the United States, a public relations exercise was launched: Waldheim was to meet every delegation of American businessmen he could find in the country. At these meetings Waldheim would praise fulsomely America's traditional support for Austria. Eventually, the American Ambassador would be forced into admitting that 'the storm was over' and that the passions Waldheim's election had aroused were a thing of the past.

The Austrian Jewry, however, remained conspicuously unimpressed by such overtures. Waldheim's sudden conversion – as it was put – to the cause of anti-Semitism should not be seen as 'absolution'. Ivan Hacker, the Israeli cultural community's spokesman in Vienna, said that it was his duty as a democrat and Austrian as well as a Jew to point out the dangerous anti-Semitic accents of the campaign. But by the autumn all did appear to be quiet and Austrians of every political persuasion settled down, convinced that the Waldheim affair could be forgotten as the parties limbered up for the general election.

Autumn in Central Europe, as anyone who has experienced this season in Austria will know, is long and mellow. Beginning in October, it runs through to late December, the trees baring themselves only in the last days of the year with the first snowfall. In spas and high mountain resorts it is the traditional time for party congresses; sated by long holidays, Austria's politicians enjoy the best time of the year planning strategy. At the Socialist Party and conservative People's Party congresses, minds concentrated on budget deficits rather than world opinion. But in the Tyrol, where the Freedom Party was gathered, more fundamental issues were on the agenda.

Innsbruck, perhaps more than Graz or Klagenfurt, epitomizes the anti-Viennese spirit of Catholic traditional Austria. Tyroleans have a long tradition – longer than anyone else in Austria – of independence. In 1809 they rose up under Andreas Hofer against Napoleon, defeating Bavarian and French troops, only to be betrayed by the compromising Habsburgs in Vienna. The picturesque city, set beneath towering peaks, was a suitable stage for what now took place. The Freedom Party, it will be recalled, had always had a nationalist tinge, but under its young leaders it had tended to pursue a more European liberalism. Personifying this, albeit on a spectacularly incompetent scale, was the party's leader and Vice-Chancellor, Norbert Steger.

Steger, the former Vienna choirboy, possessed little of the fibre which would appeal to older nationalist members of the party. What now became obvious, though, was that following Waldheim's election, Steger's stock was collapsing among younger members of the party, who appeared to be just as pan-German and right wing as the older members.

In Carinthia Jörg Haider, the charismatic local leader of the Freedom Party, had tilted for years at the 'incompetent corrupt and lazy leadership in Vienna'. It was an easy vote winner. The Frischenschlager affair had already rallied the party behind those young politicians who might be willing to dabble in Austria's brown past. For anyone who regularly observed Austria's politics, it must have been clear what was going on. Only Steger himself seemed incapable of seeing the coming storm in the Tyrolean capital.

On the last day of the party conference, a morning stroll through the old town revealed the magnificent tomb of Maximilian I in the Tyrolean equivalent of Westminster Abbey, the Hofkirche. The tomb's imposing bronze figures represent the finest German renaissance craftsmanship, and it is one of the great sights of Northern Europe. That morning, as the crisp autumn sunlight cut in shafts through the dust of the Hofkirche, there seemed an uncanny resemblance between the crude corpulent figure of Sigismund, Count of Tyrol, and the unfortunate Steger, while the trim figure of King Arthur leaning on his shield, so obviously a man of character and action, seemed to represent the energetic Haider. It was not difficult to imagine which one the rough-and-tumble rank and file of the Freedom Party would choose in a vote.

The decision to elect Jörg Haider to the party leadership took the Austrians by surprise, despite the overwhelming support he seemed to enjoy at this conference, where scenes of delirious excitement were recorded. Haider was hailed by some sections of the party as 'Hitler's adopted son', and his powers of oratory rose to the occasion with a brilliance and fire which unleashed scenes close to hysteria rather than jubilation. Steger, the outgoing leader and loser, was booed and hissed and was reminded all too crudely of his partly Jewish origins. A party elder who had supported him suffered a heart attack and had to be carried out of the packed meeting. Austrians watched their television sets, entranced by events which were pure theatre. From having been a man the Austrians and, indeed, many foreign journalists had marked down as a politician with no future, Haider was now in all but name the deputy leader of the country and Vice-Chancellor.

To his everlasting credit, Chancellor Vranitzky, perhaps because as a man reared in the more realistic world of finance he could foresee what this would mean for Austria, immediately dissolved his coalition with the Freedom Party and called for new elections. No one had looked more peeved the year before than Vranitzky when, as Finance Minister, he had had to publicly support the Freedom Party's Defence Minister, Frischenschlager, during the scandal over his greeting of Walter Reder. Vranitzky was all too aware that Austria's reputation in the world, already fragile because of Waldheim, could not carry having someone with brown shadows in the government as well.

Typically, Vranitzky's stand was unappreciated by many Austrians; they resented having more elections, or feared a great shift in the balance or power or could not see what all the fuss was about. Nothing demonstrated better the inescapable law of Austrian political life that personality and appearance are much more important than policy and ideas. The fate of Steger, who remained Vice-Chancellor until the election, underlined this. Ignored and cursed by his own party, he remained a leper until, with the election results, he retired from politics. Only those few Freedom Party politicians who dreamt of a more liberal party and of turning Nazis into democrats looked on his departure with regret.

Vranitzky's action was all the more brave given that it came less than three months after the socialists had been defeated in the presidential election by a vote of more than 7 per cent. If the disillusionment which existed over their policies had been exploited by Waldheim and the People's Party, then in the face of world opinion surely it would spell their doom.

What was so staggering to an outside observer was that within a few months of Waldheim's election a chain of events had changed the political landscape and introduced a new breed of Austrian politician who was more ambitious, more professional and more competent than the old. Vranitzky and Haider were proof that talent could be harnessed by the country. Had it not been that Haider represented the Freedom Party, his oratory and very great political acumen could have been used to serve his country in more worthy ways. The old school of Sinowatz and Steger, with a daily diet of scandals, was past. As Frederick the Great had remarked when faced with a similar wind of change after the beginning of the Seven Years War, these were no longer the same old Austrians.

During the election campaign Haider proved again and again his ability to blind Austrian voters with simple but stirring rhetoric. As the posters of him went up, depicting a sun-tanned, sharply chiselled face not unlike that of the ski-instructor of popular holiday brochures, it was clear he would make gains at someone's expense. Not at Vranitzky's, however, whose unruffled style went down very well and whose Western European experience and appearance reassured even those voters who traditionally would have voted for the conservative People's Party. This party only emphasized the inertia and complete lack of ability to adapt which characterizes the worst aspects of Austrian politics. Its leader, Herr Mock, constantly looked exhausted on the campaign trail, while attempts to portray the greying 52-year-old as a young Austrian through posters of him, top shirt button undone, skipping with teenagers, were clearly misguided.

The People's Party, which had expected to sail home on the crest of the Waldheim wave, lost seats to Herr Haider, and the socialists retained a majority. But as there was no party with an overall majority, a grand coalition had to be formed in which Herr Mock became Vice-Chancellor and Foreign Minister. As far as Waldheim was concerned, while the socialists were still in the driving seat, his party was in office after an absence of sixteen years, and the new Foreign Minister would be sure to protect him abroad. That such protection was necessary was becoming quickly apparent. Though things were quiet, an offensive by the Austrian diplomatic service to 'find an invitation for the President' had run into the sands. Everywhere in Western Europe Austrian ambassadors were being received with friendly but uncooperative replies. Western sensitivity towards the subject was most vividly displayed when foreign ministers of the states who were signatories to the Conference on Security and Co-operation in Europe turned up in Vienna and refused to meet their host. One old friend of Waldheim's, the Swiss Foreign Minister, was reported to have been begged by Waldheim to visit him. Finally, giving in 'for old times' sake', the minister assented on the condition that there would be no cameras. Unfortunately, there were, and an angry Swiss parliament demanded to know a few weeks later why the meeting had taken place.

A month later, reports in the Austrian press that his isolation was ended and that a visit to Japan had been agreed brought an angry denial from Tokyo. In order to brush up his image, Waldheim resorted to setting up an office especially responsible for the task under the guidance of Georg Hennig. For several months the office beavered away, but in May their task was made even more difficult by the news that the US Department of Justice had finally decided to place Waldheim on the watch list. Waldheim was now *persona non grata* in America and the World Jewish Congress had won its first major victory. The Austrians were rattled.

CHAPTER NINE

THE WORLD JEWISH CONGRESS AND THE WATCH LIST

From Vienna to Budapest is only a few hours by train or car or, for those inclined towards more leisurely transport, by ship down the Danube. Within days of the US Justice Department's announcement, the World Jewish Congress assembled in Budapest for an annual meeting. Despite all the similarities between Vienna and Budapest and despite the common traditions of Central Europe, for the World Jewish Congress there seemed a world of difference between the two cities.

Most of the delegates remembered with a shudder their meeting in Vienna, which broke up in dismay when the young Defence Minister Frischenschlager met the former Obersturmbannführer Reder on his repatriation to Austria. Hungary, in contrast to Austria, seemed to have an altogether more agreeable record when it came to anti-Semitism. Moreover, despite the problems in doing so as a communist country, Hungary had preserved 136 functioning synagogues and twenty-six rabbis. The World Jewish Congress made no attempt to deny that it felt very at home in the Hungarian capital, but the meeting was overshadowed by the banned President, a few hours upriver.

Within hours of the Americans' announcement, the Austrians had suddenly become aware of the Waldheim problem. It was galling to any patriot to hear a spokesman for Meese class the man they had just elected President in the same category as a common criminal. 'His name,' said the spokesman, 'will be added to the watch list. His name will be added to a look-out system to alert consular officers as to his prima-facie ineligibility for a visa to enter the United States.' The man the world trusted was in purdah.

On the train to Budapest two Austrian journalists argued over the relative merits of the decision. While one insisted that the decision was ill-advised, since it only made the Americans seem hypocritical, and that the Austrians would rally round as they always did when their patriotism was questioned, the other was convinced that Waldheim's days were numbered. 'The Austrians are not capable of defending him now; they are not Germans, they swim with the tide,' he insisted. Certainly it seemed as if two emotions were now running neck and neck among the Austrians. The first was, as predicted, outrage; the second was a discernible feeling that the situation was now really *ernst*, or serious, and that all Austrians, not just Waldheim, would suffer from this blow to their prestige.

Waldheim hastily threatened to initiate legal steps against the United States Department of Justice for barring him from the country. In Innsbruck he adopted a belligerent tone and confirmed that he was in touch with his lawyers and seeking legal advice in the United States. His lawyers were examining 'very carefully' the legal grounds for the Justice Department's decision to place him on the watch list. Austrians who feared their star was now in decline on the international stage were reassured that 'there was no question of Austria being isolated in the world'.

Chancellor Vranitzky returned from a visit to Holland and supported Dr Waldheim's call for a commission of historians to examine the war archives, adding in his inimitable style, 'It is important we do all we can here and abroad to end this rather irrational debate about our country.' At the same time the Austrian Foreign Ministry issued a statement rejecting criticism that it had been less than wholeheartedly engaged in its attempt to promote the President. Thomas Klestil, the Austrian Ambassador in the USA, had come under considerable fire when the watch list decision was announced, but had clearly been unable to do anything other than he had done, which was an exercise in damage limitation doomed to failure.

As the World Jewish Congress beamed with delight at the Americans' decision, Waldheim suddenly said – no doubt to the consternation of his lawyers and advisers – that he would sue the Congress. In particular, he would take its President, the cool, fast-talking Edgar Bronfman, to court for defamation. Bronfman had said on his arrival in Budapest that he considered Waldheim to be 'part and parcel of the Nazi killing machine'. When told of Waldheim's decision to sue, Bronfman merely replied, 'I don't take this man seriously, but if he wants to sue, let him go right ahead.'

For the Austrians the fact that the Congress proceeded to pass a unanimous vote congratulating the Reagan administration on its decision only confirmed their suspicions of a conspiracy. The Congress's headquarters in the Budapest Hilton certainly seemed to most of the Austrians present to reek of intrigue. Journalists would suddenly be approached and invited for special briefings with Mr Bronfman. Security was as tight as if a terrorist attack were expected at any moment, while the secretariat of the Congress surpassed itself in cost-cutting by issuing typed accreditation cards and overworking one or two typewriters to produce copies of the main speech for scores of hungry journalists.

Isn't it typical, an Austrian journalist remarked. Here are the wealthiest men in the world and they can't even afford a proper photocopier. Another correspondent quipped that that was precisely why these people were wealthy. The degree of the wealth may have seemed irrelevant to most journalists, but to the Austrians who had to go through a kind of Aladdin's cave filled with turquoise-bejewelled chess sets and a display of other precious artefacts, such conspicuous largess was somewhat alien. They also shuddered at the repeated demands of the Congress towards the end of its two-day meeting for the United Nations to publish its files on suspected war criminals. As we have seen, the files, which include lists of concentration camp personnel, were available to countries only on a confidential case-by-case basis, and Javier Perez de Cuellar, the UN Secretary-General, had so far refused to publish them. Out of the seventeen nations which made up the now defunct Commission which had compiled the files, only the Australians supported the motion to publish. The suppression of these files was an 'obscene perversion of justice', Elan Steinberg, an American delegate to the World Jewish Congress said. While he was confident that the files would be published soon and that the Americans would drop their objections within the very near future, gruesome details of the files were read to journalists in Budapest. No one who saw them could doubt that a spate of prosecutions involving by now very old men would result from publication. The files included lists of the entire staff of Auschwitz and several other concentration camps.

Back in Vienna, an increasingly unpopular American Embassy was besieged with inquiries as to what the watch list decision really meant. It was pointed out that Waldheim was only banned in his capacity as a private individual and that if he wished, he could visit the USA as head of state. This calmed many Austrians, though they did not ask themselves how likely such an invitation would be. Alois Mock rallied his party by accusing the Americans of using administrative measures against Waldheim which 'did not accord with a single European legal convention on evidence and proof'. Following hard on the heels of the American decision to deport Linnas to the Soviet Union for trial for war crimes, it seemed to some Austrians to smack of an arbitrary and non-judicial process which was motivated only by base instincts of revenge.

As Chancellor Vranitzky was expected to visit the United States later that month, it was clear that the issue would have to be at least discussed between Austrians and Americans at an official level. In a departure from normal conventions, the Americans magnanimously offered to send a three-man delegation to explain the case to Austrian officials. What followed was a magnificent new variation on old themes: the Americans' inability to make themselves understood to the Austrians, and the Austrians' failure to present their viewpoints rationally and logically to the Americans. The crux of the American decision to place Waldheim on the watch list was not the conviction that he was a war criminal and that this could be proved in a court of law, but that on the face of it there was a case against him, showing that he assisted or 'otherwise participated in the persecution of persons because of race, religion, national origin or political opinion'.

To explain the American position was the deputy Secretary of State in the Department of Justice, Mark Richard. To question it on the Austrian side was the former ambassador to America, Thomas Klestil, soon to be appointed Secretary-General of the Austrian Foreign Office. 'It's too technical,' the diplomat remarked after this first long session with the Americans in the Ballhausplatz. One of those present described the debates, which often reached an emotional pitch, as being 'like an argument between some of the most intelligent lawyers in the world and some of the most stupid'.

From the beginning the Austrians failed to see that the US decision was a *legal* one based on American law. The Austrians were impatient of the niceties and detail of American law and wanted instead to rush quickly into the documents which were the grounds for the prima-facie case against Waldheim. The meetings were adjourned.

Richard and the head of the Office of Special Investigations, Neal Sher, said that if the Austrians continued to want just to talk documents, they were on the way back on the next plane. After some negotiation, Klestil agreed to accept the Americans' procedure. This, however suitable for explaining a case in America or other parts of Western Europe, was sadly ill-equipped for allaying irrational and hysterical Austrian fears that the Americans were acting like mavericks in an 'unfair way'. For a start, the Americans brought no Wehrmacht documents. Furthermore, they did not offer their own 200-page Waldheim documentation or files. All their evidence would be oral.

This only confirmed the Austrians' worst fears. The Austrian newspapers had a field-day, splashing headlines which accused the Americans of acting unjustly. 'Not a single document had they brought with them, *these* Americans,' shrieked a Vienna daily. The old xenophobia resurrected itself. Austrian lawyers, albeit unwillingly, found the verbal arguments 'very impressive'. Richard and his team had been well briefed; their arguments were pertinent.

The Americans were keen to point out from the beginning that there were several precedents for their decision. In recent years a former Wehrmacht translator had been put on the list for precisely the same reasons: having assisted or otherwise taken part in reprisals against noncombatants. The Americans explained that by the Holtzman Amendment of the Immigration and Nationality Acts, to be put on the watch list Waldheim only needed to have a prima-facie case against him. The grounds for this case were well founded in the Americans' eyes. In twelve months of research the Americans had not considered the question of whether Waldheim had been a war criminal, as this is not necessarily addressed in the laws governing such decisions. Rather, it was a question of whether Waldheim fell under the terms of the Holtzman Amendment.

It transpired that there was evidence that during his career in the Balkans Waldheim had been involved in the following:

1. transportation of civilians to the SS;
2. the dissemination of anti-Semitic propaganda;
3. the deportation of civilians to concentration and death camps;
4. reprisals against hostages and civilians;
5. deportation of Jews from the Greek islands;
6. mistreatment of Allied prisoners of war.

The Americans were quick to underline that to be found to have been involved in any one of these actions was enough to be put on the watch list. They insisted that to have known about these things while serving in a Wehrmacht unit meant 'involvement'. The Americans supported each of these points with evidence.

In spring 1942 Waldheim was liaison officer with an Italian mountain division named Pusteria, which delivered 484 Bosnian civilians to the SS. The Bosnians were later taken to a labour camp in Norway. Then there was Waldheim's role at the battle of Kozara in the summer of

1942, one of the bloodiest actions undertaken by Croat and German troops against the Serbian partisans and the civilian population. There was evidence that Waldheim's honesty about his description of his career at this time could be questioned. 'His statements did not correspond to the facts,' the Americans said. According to archives of the Wehrmacht in Freiburg (RH 19Xi/81, S. 242 Bundes Archiv Freiburg), German sources recorded losses between 10 June and 29 August as:

German dead	71
German missing	8
Croatian dead	475
Croatian missing	510
Rebels dead	4735
Rebels imprisoned	12207

The German sources do not give any evidence as to how many Yugoslavs died in reprisals, but the Yugoslavs claim that more than 68,000 people, including women and children, were sent to a concentration camp.

Waldheim has revised his role at the battle of Kozara several times. At the end of March 1986, after the first allegations came to light, he explained to the Yugoslav paper *Vecernje Novosti* that although at that time he was in 'the area of Kozara', he had not been directly involved in the fighting. A few days later he corrected his statement to *Vecernje Novosti*: 'I made a mistake when I said I was in Kozara. I have analysed everything with my son and come to the conclusion that I was at that time in Pljevlja and then later I realized that this place lay geographically rather a long way from Banja Luka and Kozara where the big battle in 1942 took place.'

This seemed to put Waldheim in the clear for the moment, but as with his other haziness over his precise geographical whereabouts, it in fact only landed him further in the fire. A few weeks later the researches of the *Neues Österreich* group shattered his argument. In its brochure, entitled 'Doing his Duty', they showed that Waldheim's stay at Pljevlja had nothing to do with his participation in the Kampfgruppe Westbosnien. In Pljevlja the lieutenant was a liaison officer between the Italian Pusteria mountain division and the Kampfgruppe Bader from April 1942.

Presented with this the Waldheim defence turned again, and Waldheim's son Gerhard, after researches in his father's archives, acknowledged that a mistake had been made. On 1 August 1986 Waldheim's lawyers, Donald Santarelli and Tom Carroccio, in an 88-page deposition, admitted that 'until now a substantial factual error' had been incorporated into their defence. This, they insisted, was the result of 'mistaken translation and interpretation of an historical document'.

Contradicting earlier statements, it now emerged that Waldheim was ordnance officer 02 in the staff of the quartermaster (Ib) of the Kampfgruppe Westbosnien after all. But this position meant that Waldheim had served since the beginning of June 1942 in Banja Luka. On 31 July he, together with three other officers, including Major Gehm and the staff doctor, were transferred to Kostajnica, a small settlement north-west of Banja Luka. There, on 12 August, he was visited by a Colonel Munckel. By the end of August he had left the Kampfgruppe Westbosnien and was on his way to Salonika, where he arrived in the middle of September.

But once again, just before Christmas 1986, Waldheim felt it necessary to correct this statement in a further deposition to the Justice Ministry in Washington. This time the testimony under oath of the 77-year-old former Wehrmacht Corporal, Ernst Wiesinger, was invoked to say that Captain Hermann Plume, Waldheim's superior, at this time was not quartermaster (Ib) but a much less important supply officer (IVa). Wiesinger's testimony – he was staff writer for Plume – is of considerable significance. If it is correct, then Plume and, therefore, Waldheim were only concerned with supplies of equipment and clothing. If, on the other hand, Waldheim's original statement of 1 August was correct, then the question of deportations rears its ugly head.

The U S research team accepted Waldheim's statements of August and found Wiesinger's testimony implausible when taken in conjunction with files in the National Archives in Washington. A facsimile of the secret working documents of the quartermaster's section revealed responsibility for the deportation of prisoners. Unfortunately, as the Americans themselves admitted, the most important part of the Kampfgruppe Westbosnien's papers, including the war diary, have disappeared. This left Sher and his team with just a handful of documents, but every one of them contradicted Wiesinger's testimony.

In one, which refers to an order of 2 June 1942 and is signed by Colonel Munckel, Hauptmann Plume is described in the Wehrmacht shorthand as Ib. In this same paper the question of prisoners is also mentioned. In another document of Munckel's there is a reference to a quartermaster (Ib) who is distinguished from the supply officer (IVa). These gave conclusive proof, as far as the Department of Justice was concerned, that Waldheim had been attached to a staff responsible for deporting prisoners.

Waldheim argued, however, that the tasks of an ordnance officer (02) would not have brought him into contact with such duties. His responsibilities were the supplies and the war diary. This argument was rejected by Neal Sher. As second officer in the quartermaster's section of the unit, it seemed self-evident that he would be involved in the transportation of partisans and civilians and enemy prisoners.

The Americans also explained to the Austrians that further grounds for the decision rested on Waldheim's role in Operation Black in May 1943. At that time Waldheim was an interpreter and liaison officer in Tirana. His staff was engaged in the preparations for the operation. Sher insisted on reading the orders for the participants in Operation Black to the Austrians. The troops were to fall upon the civilian population with 'the utmost brutality' in order to deprive the enemy of every possibility of existing. Villages were to be burnt in a 'scorched earth' campaign. Waldheim, according to the Americans, must have known of this; the more so given the fact that he was interpreting between Italian and German troops. There was also the question of Waldheim's presence in Athens in the summer of 1943 as part of the German General Staff with the 11th Italian army. Following Italy's capitulation on 8 September 1943, Waldheim, on the staff, 'co-operated' with the deportation of Italian prisoners of war to labour camps. 'Co-operation', as far as the American team was concerned, included the carrying out or transmission of such orders.

The next subject the American team addressed itself to was the deportation of Greek Jews in 1943 and 1944, first from Salonika, then from the mainland, occupied originally by Italian troops, and the islands. Only in the last of these were the Americans convinced Waldheim played a significant role. That he was *actively* involved could – predictably – not be proved. But although Sher could not find a single document to verify that Waldheim had personally taken part in the transportation of the Jews from the islands, there were several documents which showed that Waldheim's staff group Ic/AO was responsible for the action.

Waldheim's claim that he did not know about the Jews on the islands looked exceptionally feeble when Sher quoted the text of a radio message written down by Waldheim, dated 15 August 1943. Waldheim's intelligence report here noted the 'Jewish committee at Joannina, a prepared centre for a rebellious movement'. German reports showed that three weeks later, after the Germans seized the Greek mainland, some 2,000 Jews were deported from the prefecture of Joannina, in 1944. Even if

Waldheim was not formally involved in this act he must have been aware of the consequences. The fact that he had always claimed, 'I hear about this for the first time', 'I swear on sacred oath that I knew nothing of these deportations', put the President's integrity further in question.

Also indicative of Waldheim's knowledge of these events was the presence of Major Hammer, who was working very near Waldheim in the Heeresgruppe E. On 21 April 1944 Hammer had ordered that the 1,600 Jews in Corfu be seized. Thereafter he was regularly informed about the situation. This and references in the war diary of Army Group E to the numbers and disposition of Jews in Greece again suggest that the problem of the Jews was one requiring considerable staff work and that Waldheim's staff unit was kept constantly informed. On 28 April 1944 orders were given for Jews to be transported in 'order to ease the shortage of supplies'.

Every week reports came through from Rhodes or the eastern Aegean, referring to the 'mixed feelings' greeting the dragging away of the Jews. On 18 May 1944 orders for the sudden transportation of Jews from Joannina arrived, as the other orders and reports from the High Command did, on the desks of Ic/AO, Waldheim's staff unit.

For the Americans this further increased the balance of evidence in favour of Waldheim's knowing about the transportation of Jews. Waldheim's lawyers rejected the argument on the grounds that Waldheim had very little contact with Major Hammer, and that he would only talk to him when he represented his superior, Lieutenant-

Colonel Warnstoff, during his absence. Otherwise Waldheim's duties took him in a different direction. Against this, the Americans insisted that a series of anti-Semitic leaflets distributed at about this time carried the stamp of the High Command Army Group E with the '03 W' and under the AO a 'Wal'. Though Waldheim swore that the 'Wal' was not his or any reference to him, he remained far from exonerated in the eyes of the Americans.

A second document also cast doubt on Waldheim's defence that his duties were 'unconcerned with such matters'. Dated 15 February 1944, it discusses the division of duties in Heeresgruppe E. According to this, as 03, Waldheim was responsible for 'personnel affairs'. Finally, Sher and his team reminded the Austrians of the massacre on the road between Stip and Kocane in October 1944. Waldheim was responsible for the reconnaissance report which led to reprisals being taken.

Given this vast amount of evidence, there was little the American Department of Justice could do but place Waldheim on the watch list. As consolation for the President, it was conceded that all officers who 'did their duty' in Heeresgruppe E also found themselves on the list. For Waldheim such a sweetener was of little value. For the Austrians the future of the one-time island of happy souls looked bleak. Austro-American relations sank to an all-time low, and at the Foreign Ministry an angry Mock thought of issuing a *démarche*.

Vranitzky's visit to Washington looked increasingly risky, but as if the problems of talking to the Americans were not enough for Vranitzky, he also had to put up with some opportunist sniping from Herr Haider. Haider denounced the Americans, played the Austrian patriotism card with energy and skill and said Vranitzky's visit to the USA was a 'plea for forgiveness'.

Once Vranitzky arrived in the USA, however, he surprised the Americans and the Austrians who followed his progress eagerly by displaying a calm, plausible and thoroughly masterly approach to the journalists' thorniest questions. He was not afraid of putting a journalist in his place when he needed to; his manner and, more especially, his very American English disarmed several critics. Even the most provincial Austrian now saw that Vranitzky was the man to help Austria in its moment of crisis. Sadly, despite the obvious success of this trip, Austro-American relations began to deteriorate even further.

The US Department of Justice may have been unimpressed by the reception its men had when they arrived in Vienna. It may have decided the time was ripe to remind the Austrians of more brown shadows in its past. Whatever the reason, before many more weeks were out, they sent the Austrians a present in the shape of a former concentration camp guard called Bartesch, who had lived in the USA since the 1950s. Bartesch was stripped of his American passport and told to leave the United States.

Though born in Transylvania when that beautiful land was already part of Romania, Bartesch belonged to the German minority which naturally looked towards Austria as its cultural inspiration. As a young man he was drafted into a concentration camp unit and posted to Mauthausen on the Danube. Here he shot a Jew who was trying to escape in the last year of the war. Bartesch never denied what he had done. Moreover, when he visited the Austrian Consul, who gave him a visa on his American passport to reach Austria, no questions were asked. Had it not emerged in the United States that Bartesch was a former concentration camp guard and that therefore the USA – rather belatedly – was withdrawing his papers (which there had been no reason not to issue in the fifties), one wonders if the case would ever have come to light in the Austrian media. In any event, it was rather ill-judged on the part of the Americans to choose 1987 to send back to Austria the man they had had no objections to in 1957. Unlike Waldheim's, Bartesch's record had clearly been known to the Americans from the beginning.

But if the affair reflected poorly on the Americans, neither did the Austrians come out of it well. It was pathetic to hear the Austrian media describe Bartesch as 'the American citizen' or the 'Transylvanian' or the 'Romanian by birth'. Nothing to do with us respectable Austrians, they hymned. One wondered whether any of these Austrian journalists had ever heard of the vast stretches of Europe which Vienna once ruled and for whose inhabitants Austria had for centuries been the fatherland. At first the Austrians tried to send the hapless fellow straight back to America, but the Americans informed every airline office in Vienna that their passenger would be turned back at the airport and that they would be fined for aiding an unwanted person to enter the United States. As so often happens with the Austrians, at this show of strength they capitulated, and Bartesch remained. He had many relations in Austria and had only a brief spell of mild incarceration before various lawyers found that there were no charges. Bartesch – the American, Transylvanian, Romanian – settled in Austria, where he belonged.

No doubt the Austrian Interior Ministry would have liked to have presented this as a more unusual example of Austria's role as a country for refugees. Unfortunately, however 'merciful' such behaviour was, it only served to underline that Austrians were not unwilling to accept concentration camp guards. This came at a time when reports indicated that Austrian gendarmes had been directed to discourage Eastern Europeans, especially Transylvanian Hungarians, from entering Austria by pretending not to understand them.

Like Walter Reder, Bartesch and, no doubt, countless others whose wartime records are far more dubious than Waldheim's are at liberty to wander around the Alpine republic. Waldheim himself made no comment on the Bartesch case, but, increasingly isolated at home as well as abroad, his staff now worked extremely hard to arrange a visit which would 'break the ice'.

One day in winter walking across the Ring to the Chancellery, one was greeted with an extraordinary sight on reaching the Ballhausplatz. Plain-clothes policemen loitered at every street corner; the ratio to passers-by must have been about fifteen to one. Everyone seemed to be a policeman, and the corpulent figures and battered mackintoshes were everywhere. It was a familiar enough sight in Bucharest, but quite unprecedented in Vienna.

It appeared that King Hussein of Jordan was in Vienna and was paying his respects to the President. Hussein, who owns property in Vienna, does not normally enjoy quite such blanket security arrangements while in the city. But this time he was delivering a very personal message to the President: an invitation to visit Jordan. This was promptly announced with glee. The ice indeed seemed to be melting.

Austrians, however, are nothing if not cynical, and it must have been apparent to Waldheim's aides that a breakthrough in Western Europe would be the only thing which could persuade their countrymen in the long term that Waldheim was not permanently isolated. Thus, one fine spring morning a month later, a startled Austria and even more amazed Europe and America heard that within two weeks the President would be paying a state visit to the Vatican at the invitation of Pope John Paul II. Waldheim could afford to be content: one bar in the cage had been prised open.

CHAPTER TEN

TRAVELLING FOR AUSTRIA

That Waldheim had scored points through the announcement of a sudden trip to the Vatican was clear by the outrage which attended it. Jewish organizations throughout America said that the Pope's action would 'irreparably damage Catholic–Jewish relations', while in the Vatican a dismayed papal press staff, in an unprecedented press conference, felt obliged to explain – for the first time in the history of the Vatican – the reasons behind the visit. They pointed out that it was not for the Pope to refuse a request to see him. The full diplomatic honours which would attend the visiting President were normal for the head of one of Europe's most Catholic states.

The Vatican visit and the later visit to Jordan did much to give the Austrians a feeling that not all the world was against them. But for those who continued to bay for Waldheim's resignation it was proof only of the President's ability, in the words of one angry Austrian, to 'export his problem around the world'.

In an attempt to extinguish such criticism, Waldheim and his advisers now launched a two-front offensive. However irrelevant it might seem to the World Jewish Congress, Waldheim was determined to press historians to support his cause. An international commission of military historians, including representatives from Israel and America, was set up to sift through all the arguments and documents. Also the Austrian Foreign Ministry finally produced the long-awaited 'White Book', which was intended to refute the allegations made against Waldheim.

The 'White Book' turned out to be – as it had to in Austria – a completely different colour: lurid, poison green. Its pages had been hastily put together and given handwritten page numbers; its photocopied documents were smudged and illegibly copied; and its English translations were riddled with spelling mistakes and typing errors. Altogether it was, even by Austrian standards, a *tour de force* of sloppy presentation. As a senior Austrian diplomat observed, 'The best thing any diplomat in an Austrian embassy can do with this book if he really cares about his country is consign it to the lowest drawer of his desk.'

At first glance the book contained much that was potentially embarrassing for Waldheim. His explanation that he had not referred to his wartime career in the Balkans in his memoirs because his British publishers (Weidenfeld & Nicolson) had demanded cuts was supported by a letter from the publishers. But the letter, while backing Waldheim's claim about the relevant passage, painted a grim picture of a self-centred man who was pedantic and incompetent in his dealings. His manuscript was 'too academic in tone'; it exceeded the required length by 40,000 words; and the editorial work was done 'under very trying circumstances'.

As Miss Alex MacCormick of Weidenfeld & Nicolson diplomatically observed in her testimony in the 'White

Book', 'The conflict between Dr Waldheim's conception of the book with ours . . . led to constant telephone calls and letters . . . while Dr Waldheim tried to expand the text (140,000 words) and I tried to reduce it to contractual length.' Even at the proof stage, Waldheim was still set on his egocentric vision of the book and wanted to add more material. But as regards his wartime career, the only paragraph to have been *omitted* was this rather self-effacing one: 'At the end of my study leave and after my leg had healed, I was recalled to military service. Shortly before the end of the war I was stationed in the Trieste area. When the German troops in Italy surrendered, I made every effort to avoid capture and reach home.' This is hardly an account of the momentous events of those days, which more than any other in Waldheim's career could justify the title of his book *In the Eye of the Storm.* With such a defence as this, one may well have wondered who needed a prosecution.

Nevertheless, as the 'White Book' remains the most detailed and comprehensive defence to date of Waldheim's career in the Balkans, it cannot be dismissed, however tempting it may be to do so. Moreover, there is much information from witnesses on the Balkan front and from pre-war Vienna which suggests that the truth is far more complicated than those who simply cry for Waldheim's blood imagine.

Miss Susanne Lederer, a Dutch fellow-student of Waldheim's at the Consular Academy in Vienna, painted a very different picture of the President from that in the Western press:

After the Anschluss (annexation of Austria by Germany), Kurt Waldheim never changed his views, but kept silent in public. In confidence, he then explained to me the sad day-to-day developments regarding the arrest of his father by the Nazis.

During the war, I stayed in contact with Kurt Waldheim. Furthermore, Kurt Waldheim twice visited me in the Netherlands during the war years: once in February of 1941, when he was stationed at the Western front; and once in December of 1942, when he was on home leave from the Balkans to continue his studies. His appearance in German uniform – as a soldier he had no other choice – caused considerable uproar as we were known as anti-German in our street, like all our neighbours were but for two corner houses, where Nazis lived. So to our 'good' neighbours we explained. The second time he appeared again suddenly having civilian clothes with him, so I showed him all the devastations the Germans had performed. Very upset about all that happened he told my mother that he only wanted to survive in order to work for peace.

He left me a photo in uniform to protect us as he knew that we were several times in danger because of our political views.

Other documents, if less personal, also shed a considerable amount of light on the confusion of loyalties during and after the war. One, issued by the district authority of Baden in November 1946, notes that 'on the basis of the *submitted documents* it has been established that Dr Kurt Waldheim does not fall within the provisions of the prohibitory law', and therefore was not eligible for denazification procedure. Another, from Dr Karl Gruber, who led Austria's major resistance movement during the war, and later became Foreign Minister, insisted that on becoming his personal secretary, Waldheim was subjected to 'thorough examination' on account of entries on his personal file relating to membership of Nazi organizations:

> After a thorough examination of this matter and the political position of Dr Waldheim towards National Socialism, I was informed that the examination had brought forth the unfoundedness of these entries and that there where [sic] no objections to the assignment of Dr Waldheim to the proposed position. I have also discussed this matter with the then Chancellor Figl who knew Dr Waldheim's family and who was, like me, aware of the fact that the whole family had been exposed to prosecution during the NS time because of 'political unreliability'.

Dr Gruber's support was tarnished somewhat in 1988 when he accused the international historians investigating Waldheim's war activities of being 'biased and Jewish'.

Another persuasive affidavit was that of Fritz Molden, the officer who had acted as go-between for the Austrian resistance movement and the Allies. This concerned detailed checks on Waldheim's career:

> The then Foreign Affairs Minister, Dr Karl Gruber, whose secretary I was at that time, in the end of 1945 gave me the order to examine, in co-operation with the Ministry of the Interior, the political past of Dr Waldheim with respect to possible membership in NS organizations. Since Dr

> Waldheim was to take on a function in the cabinet of Minister Gruber, this examination naturally had to be conducted especially thoroughly. As far as I can remember, I therefore went to see the then State Secretary in the Austrian Ministry of the Interior, Ferdinand Graf, and asked him for an examination of Dr Waldheim. Graf called upon me a few days later and told me that the examination had revealed no indication of NS connections of Dr Waldheim and that there were no charges against him.

As Molden goes on, not only were the Austrians unable to find anything on Waldheim:

> I also established contact with the CIC [Counter Intelligence Corps] and the OSS [Office of Strategic Services], the predecessor of the CIA, and concerned them with this issue. Both organizations were then enganged [sic] primarily in the pursuit of National Socialists. Both authorities told me that, based on their research, there were not the least charges against Dr Waldheim with respect to an NS past.

Molden also quotes a letter from the office of the *Gauleiter* of the Lower Danube, dated 2 August 1940, concerning Waldheim's political assessment (see Appendix, Document 2):

> The above mentioned was, like his father, a supporter of the Schuschnigg regime, and during the time of that system gave proof of his spitefulness towards our movement by boasting [*Angeberei*].
>
> The above mentioned has now been conscripted, and is said to have proven his worth as a soldier of the German army, so

that I do not oppose his admission to judicial service.

Heil Hitler!
[illegible autographic signature]

Equally powerful arguments for defending Waldheim were advanced by his contemporaries on the front. Of these, Dr Hans Haller, ordnance officer to the head of the Personnel Department of Army Group E, was particularly adamant that Waldheim had nothing to be ashamed of in his war record. In his affidavit Haller asserted the following:

> 3. During my activity with the staff of Army Group E, I was not confronted with any instance in which First Lieutenant would have been delegated to conduct prisoner interrogations.
> 4. 1st Lt. Waldheim had no power of command whatsoever in his line of duty and activity in the staff, which I was part of.
> 5. The activities of duty of Waldheim consisted exclusively in the screening and compilation of the situation information provided to him for the purpose of preparing a situation report, which was then held by the Ic officer. The materials put to his availability [sic] for this purpose were sorted out at mail entry at the staff for the first time and then upon arrival in the department Ic for the second time before they arrived at Waldheim's desk. The situation report itself was as said conducted by the Ic or his deputy. 1st Lt. Waldheim did not have a mandate for this, not even in special circumstances.

Another former Wehrmacht soldier who was at the

front at this time, but who also became a member of the Austrian resistance and was then transferred to a Croatian training brigade in Stockerau in Lower Austria gave evidence that:

> One day we received an order to compile a list of all the German members of the unit who were to be decorated with the Zvonimir Medal. I was ordered to write this list. The German personnel, some of whom had never been on the front, were awarded the medal – its value graded according to their rank. Since I had omitted my own name from the list, I alone did not receive the award.

Waldheim, it may be recalled, had been awarded the order of St Zvonimir. Unfortunately the list compiler, who is identified only as Wilhelm G., admits, 'I do not recall the exact criteria for winning the Zvonimir medal.'

A more forthcoming witness was retired Colonel Bruno Willers, who was head of operations in the German liaison staff in Athens. He was acquainted with Waldheim between July and October 1943.

> Lt. Waldheim served in all of the departments, but mainly with the Chief of Staff as an interpreter and orderly officer. At the time, Lt. Waldheim kept the divisional war diary for the Command Unit of the Staff. I remember, in particular, the time he was an interpreter during my negotiations with the General Staff Officer of the Italian army, Lt.-Colonel von Skoti, which dealt with the disarmament procedures for the Italian 11th army.
>
> Lt. Waldheim had no command authority and definitely did not play an active role in the planning, preparation or

execution of tactical and, specifically, operational actions.

Waldheim was a tactful, reserved officer, and he was highly regarded by his fellow officers.

The book also contained documents from America in defence of Waldheim. James T. Miller, a certified documents expert and consultant on handwriting to over twenty US government agencies, insisted in his affidavit that although it appeared that Waldheim may have written the initials 'KW' at the right of some reports, others, including those thought to contain the letters 'Wal' in fact were either 'Wil' or 'Wel'. Miller concluded, 'there is no resemblance between these "Wel" initials and the known writings of Kurt Waldheim and therefore no basis for identifying him as the writer of these initials'. As for the 'W' in the 03 blocks found on the anti-Semitic propaganda, Miller stated, 'Although there are some general similarities between the handwriting of Kurt Waldheim and the "W" in the 03 blocks . . . unexplained differences prevent his being identified as the writer of the initials. It appears likely that they were written by another person or persons.'

The 'White Book' wheeled out Lieutenant-Colonel Warnstorff, Waldheim's superior, who as a staff officer was head of the Intelligence Branch in Arsakli. Warnstorff claimed considerable expertise:

First Lieutenant Waldheim was my ordnance officer 03. Due to the way our staff operated, I know the responsibilities and activities of First Lieutenant Kurt Waldheim during his service with Army Group E, first in Arsakli, Greece, and

> then in Yugoslav cities Mitrovica, Sarajevo, Nova Gradiška and Zagreb, precisely.
>
> The main task of First Lieutenant Waldheim consisted of the collating and evaluation of incoming enemy information for the enemy situation report to be prepared twice daily. These reports were restricted to the strengths, activities and presumed plans of armed enemy forces, which operated in the operations region of Army Group E . . .
>
> As 03, First Lieutenant Waldheim had no power of command . . . I am not aware of a single instance where Waldheim would have gone beyond his competences in this respect. The interrogation of prisoners did not belong to the area of duty of First Lieutenant Waldheim. He only evaluated reports on conclusions from such interrogations.
>
> Although the Ic group itself was a part of the department Ic/AO, it is necessary to distinguish clearly between the tasks of the Ic group, to which First Lieutenant Waldheim belonged, and the tasks of the AO group, which was led by Colonel Hammer, the counter-intelligence officer of Army Group E.
>
> As counter-intelligence officer, Hammer only passed on those [sic] information to the Ic, which were pertinent to the enemy situation . . .
>
> My last contact with First Lieutenant Waldheim in the Wehrmacht took place towards the end of April 1945. At this time I held a small farewell event for him in Zagreb.

With regard to the interrogation of Allied prisoners of war and their subsequent disappearance, a theme pursued with particular vigour by the British MP Greville Janner, the 'White Book' quoted excerpts from German documents captured by the Allies and found in the US

National Archives. The following extract from Army Group E's war diary was held to show that Waldheim had no direct contact with the prisoners:

> 1640 Oberleutnant Waldheim informs head of General Staff that, according to news from the Air Force, our shipwrecked who found safety on Levita imprisoned and disarmed the Englishmen on the island. Major-General Winter: Please radio immediately to Lt.-General Müller: according to information as yet not confirmed, German shipwrecked who landed on Levita are said to have disarmed the English occupying force.
> 1650 Major-General Winter gives instructions to Oberleutnant Waldheim for transmittal to the Air Force that Army Group E wishes to have the prisoners of Levita picked up by Junkers aircraft and to provide the German occupation force with weapons and instruments and whatever else they need.

These entries, claim Waldheim's defenders, underline the fact that his role in the matter was 'nothing more than that of a conduit relaying messages as directed by others'. The 'White Book' goes on:

> Any information, messages or requests transmitted neither originated from Dr Waldheim nor did he participate in any of the activities which were the subjects of the messages . . . The transmission of a request from the Chief of Staff to the Air Force to transport British soldiers from Levitas to the mainland can certainly not be interpreted as 'handling of Allied prisoners'. Therefore nothing in the historical record contradicts or even calls into question Dr Waldheim's

assertion that he was not involved in the handling or interrogation of Allied prisoners or commandos.

Finally, the 'White Book' set about attempting to cast considerable doubts on the testimony of one Johann Mayer, a personnel clerk who made the following statement on 17 December 1947:

> I entered the staff of Army Group E at Thesaloniki on 3 April 1944. I was assigned as a clerk in the personnel section. At that time, the following were assigned in the command: Lt.-Col. Warnstorff of the General Staff who was the Ic officer of the Army Group [i.e. the third General Staff officer in rank]. Lt. Waldheim, whose Christian name so far as I recall was Kurt, was attached to his section; he was officially an aide-de-camp (03) but in fact he performed the duties of an Ic officer for espionage.
>
> Lt. Waldheim's job was to propose to his superior, Lt.-Col. Warnstorff, all actions of Ic and to prepare all the written reports for that purpose. These reports dealt with the question of hostages, retaliation measures and behaviour with regard to war prisoners and the civilian population. I am aware that, at the time, when we, respectively Army Group E, came from Greece into Yugoslavia – that means, a short time before that, a general order was issued according to which all retaliation measures etc. should not from now on, as in the past, depend on decisions of the field commanders and other troop commanders, but on Army Group E, that is on its Ic staff.
>
> I am aware of the fact that during the course of our withdrawal from Greece, according to which order in future retaliation measures would be moderate, so that victims would no longer be shot in a ratio of 1 : 100 but 1 : 10 and that houses would be burned in such circumstances . . .

The issuance of orders preceded, as a rule, the following proposals would be worked out by Lt. Waldheim and submitted to his superior, Lt.-Colonel Warnstorff; in case the latter agreed, he forwarded them for approval to the Chief of the General Staff, General Richberg, on whose decision the validation of such orders depended. In trivial cases, where no matter of principle was involved, Lt.-Colonel Warnstorff himself could make the decision.

This somewhat forceful evidence is held to be suspect by the compilers of the 'White Book' who persuaded Mayer's widow (Mayer died in 1972) to deposit the following affidavit:

I confirm that my husband never told me anything about First Lieutenant Waldheim and his relationship to him during the war . . .

My husband Dr Johann Mayer told me after his returning from Yugoslav prisoner of war captivity that he had been arrested then, since one was looking for a war criminal [called] Mayer, for whom he was obviously erroneously mistaken. When the wanted man was found later, my husband was released from captivity and transferred to a normal POW camp. My husband according to his narratives was repeatedly interrogated about different staff officers of Army Group E. After the war he told me that he and his co-prisoner at that time made incriminating testimony only against those comrades who had died or whom one thought to be in safety . . .

Inconsistencies in Mayer's testimonies are also highlighted in the book, which notes that, given Mayer's testimony, the Yugoslav authorities could have justifiably asked for his extradition in 1947. That they did not, for the compilers of the 'White Book', was due to these 'inconsistent and materially false testimonies'.

As to the reasons why the Yugoslavs never pursued the matter, these will be discussed in more detail in the next chapter. It may be that they considered Mayer's testimony to be no grounds for extradition. Certainly the fact that they did not take the 'appropriate steps' has been held as a key point in Waldheim's defence. Listing the grounds as to why the case against Waldheim would not stand up in a court of law, the 'White Book' insisted: 'Yugoslavia, the then prosecutor, had obviously not undertaken any steps toward further prosecution, both at the time close to the actual event, when an extradition could have been demanded from the former occupation powers in Austria, and later on.' Other reasons included:

> The general order regarding retaliation measures bears a departmental reference number from a department other than that to which Dr Waldheim belonged;
>
> Dr Waldheim was never a counter-intelligence officer as claimed in the charges; he was also never deputy department head of Ic, but an aide in that department;
>
> As an aide, he had no power vested in him to order retaliatory measures;
>
> All this must have been known to the key witness, Mr Mayer, due to his assignment as personnel staff clerk;

> Given the circumstances, consciously false testimony by this witness cannot be excluded.

In conclusion, the 'White Book' stated:

> The only basis for a bona-fide continuation of the attacks on Dr Waldheim, as well as on his credibility, would have been the presentation of valid contemporary documents or testimony proving his culpability for at least one of the many misdemeanours and even crimes of which he has been falsely accused. Given the unprecedented efforts on the part of Dr Waldheim's critics, as well as the immense quantity of documentation and testimony relating to the war in the Balkans, it is inconceivable that incriminating material would not have come to light if, in fact, he had been involved in the activities or decisions imputed to him.
>
> None of the material put forward, however, can stand the test of unbiased, professional analysis. On the other hand, all charges have been disproven beyond reasonable doubt by documents, professional expertise and contemporary witnesses.
>
> The moral and emotional aspects of the issues involved, as well as Dr Waldheim's prominence, made the demands for the application of the most stringent standards of investigation in his case understandable; by the same token, since nothing has come to light which would credibly burden him, Dr Waldheim's professional record and his unimpaired assertion of innocence, as well as the general rules of fairness, call for an end to this affair.

Significantly, the book ignored the fundamental point

that Dr Waldheim's repeated lies about his knowledge of the wartime Balkans made him an unsuitable head of state. But by the time the 'White Book' was making its way to the Austrian chancelleries throughout the world, the issue had long ceased to be one concerning a lone head of state's wartime record. The international historical commission set up to investigate Waldheim found that, if not 'actively involved' in war crimes, he had been fully aware of them. The furore surrounding this conclusion brought out all the Austrians' traditional hysteria. The Waldheim affair had reopened old wounds, which ran far deeper than the question of one man's credibility. Issues emerged which are far more important than the case of whether Oberleutnant Waldheim was a war criminal or not. It is to these we must address ourselves if the wider ramifications are to be understood and we are to begin to see what this event means for the Austrians.

CONCLUSION

WHITHER AUSTRIA?

We have discussed the problems facing the Austrians when they were confronted with Nazism and the difficulty with which any resistance was organized. We saw how a denazification programme after the war failed to impart to Austria's national consciousness that it had been more than just a victim of the Nazis. It was not, as is so frequently suggested, a question of the Austrians never having begun to pursue the tattered remnants of Nazi war criminals. Immediately after the war the Austrian parliament unanimously passed legislation concerning the prosecution of war criminals, measures for denazification and a ban on Nazi or neo-Nazi activities. Under these laws investigations were ordered against 130,000 persons; they led to 23,000 court proceedings, which resulted in 13,000 convictions. Of forty-three death sentences, thirty were carried out. More than 100,000 persons were expelled from the civil service because of collaboration with the Nazi regime. Despite this, the fateful combination of the Austrian capacity for self-deception, native *Schlamperei* and the feeling among the Allies that the Austrians were never as bad as the Germans allowed the Austrians to avoid confronting their past in any rational or objective light.

These circumstances were largely forgotten in the controversy surrounding Dr Kurt Waldheim. If the

Austrians condemned the world in a misunderstanding of what all the fuss was about, the world also misjudged Austria. Austria is as much a country of Nazis as the world's press is dominated by a Jewish conspiracy. Which is not to say that Nazis, old and unrepentant or young and misguided, do not exist in modern Austria, but to say that the majority of Austrians, however crass, anti-Semitic, unintelligent and narrow-minded, are not National Socialists and would not wish to be.

But although the Austrians cannot be condemned on this ground, it must be said that there is something very wrong with a nation which aspires to political maturity but whose politicians are unable to think of anything beyond personal or party gain. For how else is one to interpret the behaviour of the two principal Austrian forces in the Waldheim affair – on the one hand, a party which was so in fear of losing its power that it saw nothing wrong with facilitating the exposure of their opponent's murky past, irrespective of the long-term damage it could inflict on their country and on the other, a party which was happy to use the old Nazi slogan 'Now more than ever' in defending its candidate. How else may one account for all the other examples of Austrian politicians saying things which could never be tolerated in Western Europe? Waldheim, for example, explained to the *Guardian* newspaper that he saw no reason why Austria, because of its wartime record, should be treated any differently from Norway. 'No one holds the Norwegians responsible for Quisling,' he noted in one of his more memorable fatuous statements. Similarly, his former chief supporter in the

People's Party, Michael Graff, insisted that until it could be proved that 'Waldheim had strangled six Jews with his own hands, he was innocent'.

It was Asquith who remarked that the German invasion of France in the First World War through neutral Belgium was 'an act of almost Austrian crassness'. A combination of thoughtlessness, stupid indifference to the feelings of others, incompetence and a tendency to strike attitudes and to break rules may be encountered at every corner in Austria, and it is fundamentally this, not Nazism, which lies at the heart of modern Austria. It is this which led Waldheim from the beginning to dismiss the accusations against him or to ignore them. It is this which persuaded so many Austrians to ignore the moral issues involved. It is precisely this crassness which makes it easy for them to forget that wherever the Third Reich murdered, Austrians were just as well, if not better, represented in percentage terms.

To forget or to belittle the extermination of Jews, Slavs and gypsies is the form of sedative Austrians have taken for over forty years in order to retain their pride. Perhaps the Austrians need anti-Semitism to allow them to blot out their despicable behaviour during the war. The trauma of being associated with such deeds falls uneasily on a people who were until so very recently known for their contribution to higher affairs of European culture. Only those foreigners who have lived in the unreal and insincere world which is modern Vienna can understand how easy it is for a nation to commit collective amnesia. This peculiarly Viennese disability, which finds echoes throughout

Austria, has been reinforced by a no less unfortunate political tradition. We have seen how the Austrians have always preferred to be administered rather than governed, how responsibility is cloaked, how inertia and bureaucracy thrive.

It is not that Kreisky failed to turn Nazis into democrats; it is that the paternal system established in Austria after the war failed to promote respect for morals or civil courage. Every society is plagued with hypocrisy and double-dealing – in parts of Eastern Europe communism is bearable and functions only by recourse to corruption on a vast scale. That a small and relatively prosperous Western democracy such as Austria should be riddled with protection and other forms of near Byzantine racketeering is all the more regrettable.

No propaganda dominates school curricula, yet cheating in exams is considered far from dishonourable, even at the universities. No economic crisis creates shortages, yet bribes and other more subtle forms of protection are endemic. There is no serious social or class problem, yet nowhere in Europe is the word 'proletariat' used negatively with such frequency. There is no wages crisis, but as soon as the government announces small cuts in wage increases and pensions, which are already the pride of Europe, students take to the streets to demonstrate.

The older generation, which must ultimately bear the blame for such petty immaturity, sets no worthy example. A short time ago lawyers and judges in Vienna went on strike, demanding more money. Greed, immaturity, crassness, pettiness, corruption; but on the reverse side of the coin? There is (increasingly rarely) charm, certainly great warmth, hopeless frivolity and masterly improvisation. Problems which would defeat the German mind are solved in a flash by an Austrian. Shall we call it cunning, or is it resourcefulness? On balance one can no longer say that the latter cancels out the former. The failure of the Austrian education system here must take much of the blame. It has signally been unable to create a public which is not fooled by journalists, journalists who are not fooled by politicians and politicians who are not fooled by ideology. Nowhere is this more striking than in the personality and meteoric rise to power of Jörg Haider, the leader of the Freedom Party. It is Haider, not Waldheim, who is Austria's real problem in confronting its past. It is Haider who will one day wield very real political power in Austria and who belongs to the generation in whose hands Austria's future lies.

So much for Austria *infelix*. The Waldheim affair cannot be discussed, however, without some reference to other players on the international board. It is a sad but undeniable fact that the case against Waldheim was made almost exclusively by Jewish organizations. Though it has subsequently emerged that Waldheim's wartime past was investigated three times by British Intelligence and that the CIA had a file on him, it is puzzling that no government took up the thorough investigation of his past or declared its interest once the controversy became public. Yugoslavia has behaved in the most self-effacing way, given that nearly all the war crimes of which Waldheim is accused were against Yugoslavs. It should not be forgotten that Tito, the great partisan himself, decorated Waldheim for his diplomatic services after the war. Waldheim was in the Austrian Foreign Ministry at a critical time in Austro-Yugoslav relations. Frontiers were still to be finalized in southern Austria. If the Yugoslav authorities and, through them, the Kremlin needed an Austrian contact, they had the perfect candidate in Waldheim, a man whose weaknesses could be exploited very easily.

Waldheim has always denied contact with communist intelligence, but anyone familiar with the methods of blackmail and entrapment which such services employ cannot fail to think of Waldheim as an obvious choice for such tactics. His great weakness was overweening ambition – no one who has ever worked for him can deny this. The Yugoslavs had the power to shatter Waldheim's diplomatic career. They did not. It would be reassuring for the Austrians if the reason for the Yugoslavs not pursuing Waldheim was, as he himself claims, that they had no evidence against him. It would be reassuring to think that it was only a bureaucratic oversight which in 1968 allowed Waldheim, as Austrian Foreign Minister, to order his embassy in Prague to stop issuing visas to Czechs. It would be equally agreeable to think that the Russian championing of Waldheim's candidature and Waldheim's later pro-Arab stance at the UN are not part of any pattern.

But now we are peering into the abyss. Irrespective of the machinations behind the career of Austria's President, the country will be living with Waldheim for years to come.

The old favourable image of the Austria of *The Sound of Music*, where elegant officers ripped up Nazi flags and refused to be Germans, will take decades to restore, for moral renewal is remote. Ultimately it is that alone which will help Austria to achieve the mature democracy which these pages have shown still eludes it.

APPENDIX

DOCUMENT 1

7744/Y/G/557 | 19 FEB 1948

UNITED NATIONS WAR CRIMES COMMISSION

YUGOSLAV CHARGES AGAINST GERMAN WAR CRIMINALS

CASE No. R/N/684 *

Name of accused, his rank and unit, or official position. (*Not to be translated.*)	Kurt(?) WALDHEIM, Oberleutnant. Abwehrofficier with the Ic - Abteilung des Generalstabes der Heeresgruppe E from April 1944 until the capitulation of Germany. (F.25572)
Date and place of commission of alleged crime.	From April 1944 - May 1945. All parts of Yugoslavia.
Number and description of crime in war crimes list.	II. Putting Hostages to Death. I. Murder.
References to relevant provisions of national law.	Violation of Articles 23 b & c, 46 and 50, of the Hague Regulations, 1907, and Article 3, para. 3 of the Law concerning Crimes against the People and the State, 1945.

SHORT STATEMENT OF FACTS.

Oberleutnant WALDHEIM, the German Abwehrofficier with the Ic. staff of the "Heeresgruppe E", headed by General LOEHR, is responsible for the retaliation actions carried out by the Wehrmacht units in Yugoslavia, inasmuch as the "Heeresgruppe E" was involved in directing the retaliation orders issued by the OKW. Thus the Ic. staff of the "Heeresgruppe E" were the means for the massacre of numerous sections of the Serb population.

TRANSMITTED BY YUGOSLAV STATE COMMISSION : [signature]

* Insert serial number under which the case is registered in the files of the National Office of the accusing State.

13th February, 1948.

(6136) Wt.P.2134/27 5m. 2/46. C. & Co. 745(P)

DOCUMENT 2

Nationalsozialistische Deutsche Arbeiterpartei

Gauleitung Niederdonau

Personalamt

Abteilung: Politische Beurteilung

Vertraulich!

Unser Zeichen u. Zahl in der Antwort unbedingt anführen!

An den
Oberlandesgerichtspräsident,
W i e n , I . ,Justizpalast

Unser Zeichen: Pe-Sch./C. 32327 Ihr Zeichen: P.A. 89/40

Betrifft: Politische Beurteilung

Wien, den 2. August 1940
IX, Wasagasse 10, Fernruf A 19-5-50 bis 57
Briefanschrift: Wien IX, Postamt 66, Postschließfach 139

Name: W a l d h e i m Kurt

Geburtszeit: 21. 12. 1918 Ort: Wördern

Wohnort: Tulln, Straße: Wildgasse 10

Der Genannte war, wie sein Vater, ein Anhänger des Schuschnigg Regi[illegible]
und hat in der Systemzeit durch Angeberei seine Gehässigkeit zu
unserer Bewegung unter Beweis gestellt.

Der Genannte ist nun zum Militärdienst eingezogen und soll sich al[illegible]
Soldat der deutschen Wehrmacht bewährt haben, sodass die Zulassung
zum Justizdienst von mir nicht abgelehnt wird.

H e i l H i t l e r !
Der Leiter des Gaupersonalamtes:

[signature]

[Stamp: Nationalsozial. Deutsche Arbeiterpartei — Personalamt — Gauleitung Niederdonau]

INDEX

INDEX

INDEX

INDEX

INDEX

INDEX

INDEX

INDEX